L.A. WOMAN

by Eve Babitz

SIMON & SCHUSTER PAPERBACKS
New York   London   Toronto   Sydney   New Delhi

FOR US ALL

Simon & Schuster Paperbacks
An Imprint of Simon & Schuster, Inc.
1230 Avenue of the Americas
New York, NY 10020

Copyright © 1982 by Eve Babitz
Introduction copyright © 2015 by Eve Babitz

All rights reserved, including the right to reproduce this book or portions thereof in any form whatsoever. For information address Simon & Schuster Paperbacks Subsidiary Rights Department, 1230 Avenue of the Americas, New York, NY 10020

This Simon & Schuster trade paperback edition October 2015

Simon & Schuster Paperbacks and colophon are registered trademarks of Simon & Schuster, Inc.

For information about special discounts for bulk purchases, please contact Simon & Schuster Special Sales at 1-866-506-1949 or business@simonandschuster.com

The Simon & Schuster Speakers Bureau can bring authors to your live event. For more information or to book an event contact the Simon & Schuster Speakers Bureau at 1-866-248-3049 or visit our website at www.simonspeakers.com.

Manufactured in the United States of America

10 9 8 7 6 5 4 3 2 1

Library of Congress Cataloging-in-Publication Data is available.

ISBN 978-1-5011-3272-8
ISBN 978-1-5011-2451-8 (ebook)

PREFACE TO THE NEW EDITION

At the time I wrote *L.A. Woman*, I thought that it was going to be the book that took over the world. Ya know, that got me everything. That everything in my life would finally go my way. It came out in 1982—the exact same time John Belushi was killing himself at the Chateau Marmont. I had been trying to get along with John Belushi for a long time. My agent sent me to New York to write about Belushi and get an in at *Saturday Night Live*, but I didn't know that at the time. He lived in a cement bunker and, you know, was famous for not being very much fun, except for his skits and everything. I tried to but could never get around him, because he was surrounded by guns and cement bunkers.

The person I ended up influencing instead was Steve Martin—who is also from the West Coast—so maybe I had more of a chance with him. I was the one who suggested that he wear that white suit. I got the idea from a 1906 Jacques-Henri Lartigue photo of a man in a white suit on the beach in Cannes titled "Cousin Caro." Lartigue took these photos when he was ten years old. He started when he was seven and continued taking them throughout his life till he accrued 250,000 of them. The day after his wedding he took a photo of his wife on the toilet. It's titled "Bibi," which was his nickname for the high-society Madeleine Messager, mother of his only child. She's smiling, because she knows it's for fun. So the guy's funny and that's what inspired Steve Martin, because he "got" Lartigue and became an immediate fan. Lartigue kept taking pictures of his family and they are now on sale at the Museum of Modern Art.

I told Steve Martin that everyone else was going for darkness, but darkness doesn't pay off. I was the one who convinced Steve with that picture. I tried to convince the Eagles to wear white suits, too, but their reaction was, "No way!" They would have looked good! Don Henley eventually wound up wearing white suits in the '80s. So did the guy who was married to Melanie Griffith. Don Johnson. Remember that *Miami Vice* thing? I mean everybody wore white suits. I finally got my way. Or they wore pale, incredible pastel colors. I totally got my way!

Let me tell you: when *L.A. Woman* came out, it had the perfect title. Then Jim Morrison stole the title for his album. But I *am* the "L.A." woman! I had some help from my friend Diane Gardiner, who was a publicist. She publicized me nonstop. She just quoted all my funny remarks and they wound up in *Rolling Stone* and that's why people wanted to meet me. So Diane kind of made me famous. Her own remarks were even funnier, but she kept a lid on it. That's how all that happened. So, when *L.A. Woman* came out, I was just positive that I was going to take over the world.

I got reviewed in the *New York Times*. I thought they would "get" me, even if

PREFACE TO THE NEW EDITION

I'm from Los Angeles. So with *L.A. Woman* I thought they were going to get me that time and just publish everything in the book, stick excerpts in the paper and it was going to be just great! But the critique of my book was titled "A Dull Girl." I hate the *New York Times*! I thought it would be wonderful. P. J. O'Rourke didn't like me. I couldn't believe it—a bad review in the *Times*! It went against all my principles. It was just awful. The truth is, they only get me when I haven't written a book in like ninety years, then they write a huge article about me and say how great I am in the Style section. But if I write a book they're like, "Oh, this is horrible!" Unless I write nonfiction. Then the *New York Times* likes me.

So, I told everybody I was going to kill myself. But I woke up rested, damn it! After sleeping two days, I was up for eight. I was up with my mother. We were drinking vodka and couldn't fall asleep. My father had also died, so we just went on a vodka bender. My mother managed to get a doctor to shoot her up with sedatives so she could sleep. But I had to take all these pills. I think it was Thorazine left over from my father's deathbed. Most addicts kill themselves by just trying to get some sleep. I've always had an iron constitution and could never do it. That's when John Belushi immolated himself in the Chateau Marmont. I was staying there at the same time, trying to kick drugs. Steve Martin and Michael Elias were paying for my stay. Carl Reiner said this thing: "Don't all those drugs disguise your symptoms?" I thought that was the purpose. I had all these symptoms and, you know, they gotta be disguised. Like boredom. Or the usual alcoholic thing, like bad excuses.

I just totally drove every person crazy. Even Paul Ruscha said I had to quit. And Paul never says anyone has to quit. Because codeine. That's the worst, most boring, and horrible drug. It had sabotaged all my relationships. Paul had to suffer with pain and misery because of the way I dated him. I was always on one drug or another. I thought, Well, if Paul can't stand it (because Paul loves everybody no matter what they do or how horrible they are), I should consider getting sober.

And codeine makes you obnoxious . . . on three continents. I went on a last horrible binge and fired everyone important in my life. I didn't realize they were trying to help me. I was so paranoid I thought everyone was against me. And that was just the codeine. I had to thank P. J. O'Rourke for the slashing review, because I owe my sobriety to him. It was either kill myself or go to Alchoholics Anonymous. The usual choice. I did thank him through friends, because that bad review got me sober. I ultimately met him and liked him, because calling me a "Dull Girl" was actually pretty funny.

—*Eve Babitz, October 19, 2014*
Transcribed and edited with the assistance of Alexandra Karova

L.A. WOMAN

Are you a lucky little lady
in the city of light.

—Jim Morrison
"L.A. Woman"

ONE SUMMER MORNING while I was still a virgin though my virginity was on its last legs, I woke up and didn't want to go to New Jersey. It wasn't fair that they wanted me to go to New Jersey; I didn't want to go—I was seventeen and no seventeen-year-old L.A. woman would go to New Jersey if she could get out of it, especially a seventeen-year-old with a boyfriend like mine—a dreamboat who was twenty-five, was under contract to Fox as a leading man, black wavy hair and blue eyes, his father a French leading man who'd once starred in a tearjerker with my Great Aunt Golda and made a million dollars which he lost on a misadventure. Anybody who went to New Jersey just to visit Aunt Helen, I supposed with outraged sensibilities, would have to be nuts. Aunt Helen was nuts to have moved to New Jersey at all, and she was really insane inviting decent L.A. people to visit her on the fucking East Coast.

But my father and mother kept up their demand, even if I did remain in L.A., about the people they would allow me to remain with. I refused hands down. Not my grandmother, period—I mean, staying with my grandmother would be like not being in L.A. at all. My Aunt Goldie's place was big enough but my cousin Ophelia had been such a drag in those days and gone to such lengths to antagonize her new stepfather by leaving joints around in 1960 where he could see them that he'd become embittered against the entire younger generation of Lubins before my sister Bonnie or I even had a chance to try our hand. I wouldn't stay with the people across the street who'd been there while I was growing up and whose daughter Shelly Craven was my age and with whom we have everything outwardly in common, because for one thing we didn't forgive them—they were Stalinists and a line of blood was painted right down the middle of Foothill Drive once they moved in when I was six—and besides, they weren't home, they were in Rome. Not that I myself wouldn't have forgiven them for being Stalinists—what *I* didn't forgive them for was playing Pablo Casals on the record player and having that melodrama going on in the middle of the afternoon as Molly Craven's token of cultural refinement. And none of my friends, like Franny Blossom, were people whose families my family would put up with—although Franny's house, God knows, was a rambling mansion and the whole guest wing was empty since Franny's "uncle"—who wasn't really an uncle but who drank as much as her father and mother and thus was a dear family friend —had gone down to Rosarito Beach fishing for three months. But ever since Franny's father had taken a beebee gun out and begun shooting it at a brass Liberty Bell above the fireplace on the mantel, my mother declared they were "trash" and once she said that, spending even one night was asking for the moon. So it looked like I was going to New Jersey and going to have to spend an entire month on the fucking East Coast.

But I knew I wasn't even though the next morning was when the plane was leaving. I knew something would save me.

I never would have imagined it would be Lola. Even though once before she slept on our living room couch when she and Luther had a fight and she drove straight down from San Francisco in six hours like a demon, back in the days when it took eight hours for any sane person to drive down.

Yet the moment I saw that intensely dark red hair I knew it was Lola.

Lola had come.

And Lola would understand perfectly why a seventeen-year-old virgin going to summer school at Hollywood High would rather not go to the fucking East Coast for a month. Of all my parents' friends, Lola was the only one who, even though she was almost beyond her fiftieth birthday, was still

L.A. enough to realize that you don't leave anyone with a smile like my new boyfriend Claude's for a whole month and expect him to be there when you got back—especially once I showed her his picture, which I happened to have with me when I explained this to her at 6:45 A.M.—and especially when I wasn't even fucking him before I left so he'd have something to remember me by. Bleaching my hair blond and looking like Sheena, the queen of the jungle, which was how I looked, wasn't enough, tan or no tan. I simply had to stay in L.A. and learn how to go down on him. But I'd never learn to go down on anyone if Ophelia didn't tear herself away from the Westlake School of Music and her junkie jazz musicians, which was her idea of fun. And Ophelia promised to tear herself away on Saturday but by Saturday I'd be in New Jersey. And it was something she had to explain in person. Every time she began even attempting to explain on the phone, we both cracked our heads on the floor from falling down and wept tears of depraved laughter. But I didn't need to tell Lola about all of that, I knew, all I had to do was beg her. Keep it simple.

"You're here," I said, waking Lola up.

"Yes," she agreed, painfully—she'd gotten to L.A. at 2:00 A.M.

"Please, Lola," I begged, at 6:47 A.M., "you've got to stay."

"Well, I—" She laughed. Since she never drank, she never woke up with hangovers and waking up was much easier for her than it was for Franny's parents.

"Stay with me," I said, shooting my picture of Claude smiling straight into my pitch. "For a month, Lola. Oh, please. Please! Can't you?"

"A month, why I—" Lola said, her mouth dropping open —but smiling—still insane enough by her fiftieth birthday to think this was a good idea basically. Besides which, she could not resist begging.

"They want me to go to the fucking East Coast!"

"That's right," she said. "To visit Helen."

"But *I* don't want to go," I explained, "I want to stay here" —she looked at Claude's picture, her eyes widening—"with Claude."

"He's a doll," Lola said.

"Of course," I admitted, "it is touched up. The studio didn't like his nose like it was. But otherwise he's really this way."

Lola pulled her reading glasses out of her purse beside the couch and scrutinized Claude's face with more objective detachment. I waited, not breathing. Of course, Claude's black wavy hair from being French wouldn't go against him. They all had black wavy hair back in those days, back when they were dancing and touring with Teretsky, marrying the wrong people. All the wrong people marrying each other had black wavy hair and the absolutely impossible men had the same kind of grin beaming ravenously out of Claude's autographed eight-by-ten glossy. So surely Lola would save me and stay while I perilously endangered my future, wrecked the vacation, and threw away the possibility to travel someplace halfway decent and see a Real City—New York—finally, which all my life I'd been told I had to do. For a bloodthirsty smile like Claude's, combined with how black his wavy hair was, threw the whole fucking East Coast into shadow. For compared with the trouble I could be in in Hollywood over the next month, all the evil companions I might fall in with in New York just paled. In fact that summer, if I'd been asked, everything paled by comparison to me then when I thought of going anyplace outside L.A. Just bothering to go someplace other than Santa Monica was incomprehensible when I could just wake up every morning at dawn, yank on my bathing suit still on the floor from the night before when I'd yanked it off, hurry down to Hollywood and Gower to catch the 91S bus down Hollywood Boulevard and then Santa Monica Boulevard to Beverly Hills and transfer to the 83 going straight out to the beach until finally there I'd be, at 8:00 A.M. or so, able to feel the cool sand get warm as the morning sun glazed over the tops of the palm trees up on the palisades while waves of the ocean crashed down day after day so anyone could throw himself into the tides and bodysurf throughout eternity.

"Your poor mother," Lola sighed, resigned.

"She said I had no one to stay with," I said, determined. "She *has* to let me. If you're here, she *has* to."

"Well," Lola said, "it couldn't hurt Luther to know I can stay away for a month. But you tell your mother. It has to be okay with her, you know? Gee, I never imagined I'd be staying here with you a whole month—and in the same neighborhood as me when I was growing up. You know, our old house isn't far from here."

"Oh, Lola, thank God you've come," I cried, although I'd known something had to save me—of course, I never would have dreamed someone as good as Lola, my parents' only halfway-up-to-date friend from the olden days, would be part of the deal.

I mean in those days, as far as I was concerned, all the Trotskyites and Stalinists and Republicans and Democrats and anyone else wearing a suit on the cover of *Time* magazine because of politics could go jump in a lake, and yet somehow, in the very midst of it all, there stood Lola. Picketing. Great legs, a figure which, when I was seventeen, I watched men drive into telephone poles over, a bizarre use of earrings, an altogether Cleopatra-girl slink to every move in her whole body, a demonically objective attitude about sizing things up and speaking her findings with a voice touched with nothing more than a glow of detached amusement over details she'd recount, laying to waste listeners, speechless when she told them, "Oh, didn't you know, she and her father bathe together. How old do you think she is? Thirty-seven. The mother, you know, she died when the girl was only a child. No one, I guess, wanted to tell him—or her —I mean *bathing!* Together. Or am I too old-fashioned?"

But of course she had never been old-fashioned enough to most of the people my father knew when political criteria were his pride and joy, although oddly enough in the end she was the only one we ever really wanted to see after all. Because old-fashioned she never became.

AND BY THE TIME I saw her the summer I was forty she still really hadn't seemed to become old. There she was—Lola—in this slinky turtleneck paisley jersey dress at seventy-two, leaving cars crashed into loud accidents commemorating her visits. Imagining how she once must have exploded and hissed and crushed through piles of men back when she was twenty-three or seventeen isn't that difficult. Seen from behind, Lola still makes seventeen seem possible. It's just when she turns around and speaks German like her mother that you can guess she's nearly fifty and still be only twenty years off. From behind, you could make a mistake of half a century. The lynxy little pout in her walk, the elbows so trimly neatened at her sides, the self-consciousness in her feet like a girl unused to such high heels yet—from behind she could easily be mistaken for a teenager out for danger, any kind of danger she can find. Lola from behind looks very capable of stirring up trouble, trouble like nobody ever hoped to see.

Trouble was Lola's middle essence.

It kept her back straight and her chin high and her expectations prepared for everything, for fathers and daughters who were thirty-seven no matter what they did in bathtubs.

At least everything except Sam.

Of course so far the worst person in Lola's milieu was Lola herself and it seemed to her, perhaps, that she had to do all the heartbreaks in town and invent everything herself.

Whereas once she met Sam Glanzrock, she could relax.

Someone who didn't even try and hide his ravenous appetites by smiling, not a single smile did he smile for a camera in all those years, not even so much as a bloodthirsty veiled transparent trick smile.

All that remains of same from Lola's photographs of those days is a weird suspicion. Not anything you would know was wrong.

It was just that Sam's hair was light brown, curling light brown hair.

He hadn't even bothered to hide under black wavy hair like in those days they all had. That's how much trouble Sam was.

(But I would know by the summer I was twenty-three when I met Jim what it was like having to be the one who breaks hearts, who causes trouble, who invents everything and is the worst, myself—but then anyone who saw Jim that night would have realized that I was looking for trouble myself.

"Let's go," I said, "fast."

"Uhhhhhh . . . where?"

"To my place, *now*—quickly, let's go now." Of course, anyone who saw me that night and had taken one look at Jim would have known I was safely aboard a raft heading over Niagara Falls. That night I was twenty-three and a daughter of Hollywood, alive with groupie fervor, wanting to fuck my way through rock'n'roll and drink tequila and take uppers and downers, keeping joints rolled and lit, a regular customer at the clap clinic, a groupie prowling the Sunset Strip, prowling the nights of summer, trying to find someone who promised I should, if I didn't stay away, only run into trouble, endangering my life.)

"How beautiful," Lola remarked, dragging out the vowels in beauty so that it lingered in my ears. "How damn well fucking beautiful this man's face is. And what a man, too. Isn't that marvelous how he still is a man? A man with that hair and a face—and so beautiful—but there's no doubt in my mind that he's heterosexual, not one."

We stood looking at his photograph like we were always looking at photographs when I visited Lola in San Francisco, and he gazed back—a gaze that meant nothing but trouble. And Jim gazed back at us—only by then I was thirty and he was dead.

"Didn't he . . . ?" she asked.

"In Paris," I said. "Too."

"How interesting," she said pleasantly, turning to a photograph of me when I was ten. "Oh, look," she cried, "you, when you were still a virgin. To think, I actually knew you when you were seventeen. What was the name of your boyfriend then?"

"Claude," I said, proud I remembered.

"**Y**OUR POOR MOTHER," Lola would remark like a lament throughout the month she stayed with me. Her voice trying to sound shocked but managing only to well up with detached amazement and then vaporize into a mist of nostalgia from the days when Rudolph Valentino's flaring nostrils in *The Sheik,* when the flashcard said "Must I be valet as well as lover?" were enough to make her come.

"Every time he said that to her, his nostrils would catch —and I would have to go relieve myself. Both physically and manually . . . I was so involved with that man."

So it was a lot better than whatever was in New Jersey. And I was a virgin when my parents returned, more or less, but not by the next weekend.

"Spit," Ophelia concluded, "that's the whole trick to giving head. Just spit." She had already showed me how to keep the grip light enough to keep the outer skin moving over the inner part. And she'd showed me how to do it so I didn't have to count on my mouth except for spit . . . and by Saturday afternoon Claude said it worked.

"That's fan*ta*stic!" he said.

"Oh, it's just spit," I said.

"No," he said, "no really, that is fan-fucking-*ta*stic!"

"Thank you," I said.

Spit was my specialty. Spit I could understand. Spit was so easy.

A T THE AGE OF FIVE Lola was brought by her family to California, along with the German silverware, the mahogany tables, the twenty-four dining room chairs, the lace tablecloths, the candelabra, the servants, from the home with a clothes hamper chute where when the cloth used for Kotex in those days was soiled, you just lightly tossed it down the little wall door and one week later it was returned to you nice and clean and neatly folded by some woman who came once a week to launder, a woman nobody ever saw— or at least Lola never even remembered. Until she ran away from home at the age of twenty-six to join a Martha Graham-type traveling modern dance troupe and became radicalized into a Trotskyite, she lived in that house with that furniture and for a long time, though she refused to speak that Berliner German they spoke at home to keep the tone up and the servants in Mars where they belonged in 1911.

It wasn't as though a lot of German silverware and candelabra weren't already out in Southern California by the time Hein Vogel, Lola's westward-destined mother—one of those Jews too elegant to have left before any pogroms squeezed her out like my grandmother's exit from Kiev—arrived, it was just that most of it was in Pasadena on North Orange

Grove Drive. The mansions in Pasadena even today are perfect for trainloads of European treasures brought from the
Midwestern fortunes—the Bambols, the Wrigleys—coming
to California for "the climate." Because if you were from the
Midwest, and you wanted to breathe air that wasn't all taken
up by the fortunes breathing in the Newport Beach-style
mansions, Henry James tablecloths, and already organized
society which wasn't going to let anyone in until endless
formalities transpired, then "the climate" of California, the
orange groves, the purple mountains' actual visible majesty
—the San Gabriel Mountains there, brightly purple—was a
good place for your servants to polish your teapots.

Perhaps Lola's German Midwestern fortune made from
stockings was refused in Pasadena because it was Jewish
and that's why it all had to come to Hollywood and that's
why Lola was raised in the middle of Hollywood during the
twenties with Hollywood Boulevard four blocks away; the
Hollywood School for Girls, the private school she attended;
Jean Harlow sitting next to her in class, Jackie Coogan, the
only boy and the school mascot, while at home she was
strictly bound to a classic Germany, a Germany of violin
practice two hours a day, of culture, of table manners that
got Bobby Hall—one of those Panthers of the sixties whom
she traveled with when she married Luther, her black second husband—so mad he shot a hole through her dining
room ceiling. I mean Lola eating ribs with a knife and fork
was just too much for him. But Lola, who was sixty by then,
could never have picked something up with her fingers—
after all her mother, then ninety-four, was still alive even if
it was in Honolulu (that woman really meant West) and even
though Lola was now officially into The Movement with a
vengeance, she just wasn't about to not use silverware.

Of course it was nothing to be too much for the Black
Panther Party when you're sixty if you've been too much for
the Hollywood School for Girls when you were fifteen.

She'd go to school there in 1926 dressed in her navy blue middy outfit and wait till school let out to change into a black skirt slit up to her thigh and a lot of blood-red lipstick smashed on the front of her face, so she could go out onto Hollywood Boulevard and try and pick up guys, trying to look older than a schoolgirl yet still unable to quite look old enough by then. Even though the Hollywood School for Girls believed the worst, Lola dropped out before she could graduate so as not to spread sin around the virgins in her class. L.A. It was impossible for her strict German upbringing to stop Lola from being too much. For L.A. women became L.A. women if they got there young enough, no matter what they had been born into.

When Lola was sixteen, her mother gave Lola a Model T Ford, a reward because Lola won the state violin gold medal —though how Lola focused herself into the discipline it takes to practice a violin during the Hollywood School for Girls is simply paradoxical enough for some L.A. woman like her to prove was possible.

The Model T Ford gave her exactly everything. She could drive down Sunset Boulevard, which in 1927 when she began taking the car to the beach wasn't much of a street at all and still isn't, though at least today it's paved.

Lola became a muscle beach aficionado, the top of four layers of musclemen—the girl with her arms raised in graceful triumph, wearing a horrible black wool bathing suit which did purposefully Bermuda shorts-type things to her gorgeous thighs and crowded her 36DD breasts into squashed-out spongecakes. The neckline was modesty itself and it was necklines like these that were probably responsible for people, the minute they could, turning into Jean Harlow by the thirties and letting the devil take the hindmost.

Mountain climbing—in those days, all you had to do in Hollywood was go outside to go mountain climbing—was

Lola's idea of where to take boyfriends and get pregnant and by the time she was nineteen she'd had three gold medals for violin state champion and four abortions, her life having finally, I suppose, proven that you can't go around being an L.A. woman and expect society not to notice when your bowing begins to sound a little off—not screechy, naturally but, well, she simply wasn't gold medal material finally, and they gave her a silver one, second prize. My father got the gold one. Even though Lola insists that my father's tone was then and always has been enough to make you leave the room.

"Mort," she says to my father, the minute he tries to play anything in front of her for as long as I can remember, "for God's sake! Not more Bach!"

And he looks around like a cat does when it pretends it wasn't doing what it just did that you caught it at, and was really licking its foot, or wondering if it were going to rain.

Lola and my father never saw anything in each other. My father would never have liked any woman crazier than my mother. And as for Lola—looking at a particularly outstanding old photograph of her standing beside this six-foot-tall extra who looked like a Hindu (as he was billed in his mystic-prince capacity for those who wanted a "reading"), both Lola and he wearing this rattan shadow falling across what would have otherwise shown them to be as naked as you thought—Mort was simply too square.

From the beginning, from the time she was standing outside that mountain cabin and she was wearing her Cleopatra haircut which she wore all her life, turning it oranger and oranger with henna as time went on until today Colette would have tripped if she saw her, Lola's preferences weren't socially bogged down. And a trust fund kept her from letting what she wanted get in the way of wolves at the door, for wolves never threatened her door and she never had to turn to the idea of respectability just to tide herself over for a decade or two until she could figure out how to indulge her flagrant tastes for the out-of-the-question. Or for men who, English mothers have always told their daughters, simply "won't do."

Even she, Lola's mother, didn't seem to get overburdened by the problem of men who "didn't do," once her only husband's brisk demise allowed her to pack up and leave for L.A.

"Nobody ever knew why Hein was such a rebel," Lola said. "The family wanted her to take the three of us home to Berlin and be brought up with the better things. Minneapolis, anything in America, was Greek to them. And when she came out West, they sent this friend of the family, this doctor called Frederik, to marry her and take her back."

A photograph of Lola's mother, Hein, looking like a battle-ax from the Queen Victoria understanding of the word, dressed in a Red Cross Volunteer Aide's outfit with some kinds of medals attached to her jacket, which meant she was a general or something gruesome like that, her hair hidden behind a nurse's nun-type headdress, her overbearing bosom completely making Lola's and mine both pretty much as hers was, except that we weren't battle-axes, forcing your eyes to look elsewhere from obviousness.

Beside her stood Frederik, a delicate Berliner Jewish intellectual who found himself spending the rest of his life in the Biltmore Hotel in downtown L.A. (for the first few years) and then, in a house nearer Hein in Hollywood, wooing her as best he could into whatever it was they did.

"They used to give musicales," Lola told me. "They'd invite the whole Berliner community over on Sundays and she would play the cello and he would play the oboe—"

"The oboe!" I cried.

"That's right." Lola shook her head.

(As anyone with a knowledge of orchestra instruments knows, playing the oboe for longer than two years makes you go insane.)

One time the musicale was a special fundraiser—though since Lola was nineteen at the time and it was 1930, what the worthy cause would have been even Lola can't remember (usually it was Flanders Field-type orphans her mother leaned toward). This particular night Lola had to get all dressed up in a taffeta and net powder-blue formal which came down to her feet and stockings, a garter belt, the works.

"And I was to play Mendelssohn's violin concerto—my first really Berlin debut," Lola remembered. "Only even though I could play it fine in public in front of judges—playing in front of all those women, they all looked like her, you know, Hein—and all those men who looked like Frederik, so sensitive and delicate—I just stood there. I couldn't remember one note. And they just sat there, politely. And I just stood there. God."

"How long did you stand there?"

"Five minutes," she sighed.

"Oh, Lola, come on, not five whole minutes. Not five! They wouldn't let you just stand up there for five whole minutes and not play a note."

"My friend timed it," Lola said. "She began looking at the clock at eight-fifteen and watched me run out of there—I left the fiddle on the stage—at eight-twenty. Precisely. And we've always been very precise."

Lola ran down the street to where her current boyfriend lived in a rooming house, rattling his window and insisting that he meet her at the corner. The "corner" was right at Beechwood and Franklin, which, today, is two blocks from where I grew up and is three blocks from where my father and mother's latest home is. (That particular neighborhood in Hollywood has always been so hard to shake that when my parents sold their house—the one I grew up in—and moved to Europe, they finally couldn't take it anymore; they missed too many things about L.A. that Rome and Paris and

Heidelberg just don't offer—they missed winters you could gloss over, I think, mainly; they got one just like it a few blocks away. It was larger than the one I grew up in but otherwise just like it, so whenever I go home things don't seem to have shrunk, like other people's houses do when they return, or like my grammar school seemed to when I wandered through it once as an adult. Returning to L.A. my parents couldn't think of the city as anyplace other than that part of Hollywood, near that corner of Beechwood and Franklin.)

The guy, whose name Lola thinks was Ted Kovokovitch (a Yugoslavian in California to plant grapes), met her within seconds.

"And there, right at that corner—you know?—I pulled up that damn taffeta and net skirt, pulled down those awful cotton drawers she always had us wear—and we—"

"You *didn't!*" I cried.

"Yes. Twice."

"But there's a street lamp!" I said.

"Is there?" Lola asked, frowning a moment. "There wasn't one then. All we had to worry about then was the Dinky."

"The what?"

"The Dinky," Lola said. "That little railroad train they used to have going up Canyon Drive. Harold Lloyd and Buster Keaton—all those western pictures they made up at the end?—they'd carry the stars and all the extras right past Hein's front window. It was the most amazing thing, looking out through all that Queen Victoria massive power of our living room—the drapes alone, my God, they must have weighed twenty pounds of velvet and lining and interlining, each panel—through the torrey pines that grew in our front yard, and there, going past on this tiny little car, not anywhere as big as a streetcar, that's what they called it, the Dinky, would be this face—this face everyone in America knew. Everyone, that is, except mother. Or any of her friends. But of course Mother wouldn't even allow the servants to go to the movies, she thought them so immoral. And I have no idea where she thought we lived."

"So the Dinky was all you were afraid of?" I asked.

"All *he* was afraid of, you mean," Lola insisted, "I was an animal."

"Well," I said, "I was *worse* than an animal."

"I beg your pardon?" she asked, the summer I was seventeen.

"Well, remember that dog Tango we used to have when I was ten or eleven?" I asked. She nodded her head. "Well, Tango and I began having an affair on the bathroom floor, sort of—not that he deflowered me or anything, I mean I did have some sense of the fitness of things, but you know I did let that Tango lick me every time I could lock us in the bathroom and lie down. The tiles were so mint green, Mother had just had it done. Anyway, I had to give him away."

"Don't tell me your poor mother found out?" Lola cried.

"No, it was worse," I said, "it was worse. You see, he began waiting for me to come home from school or the beach —he'd wait there by the window day and night. I was afraid they'd get suspicious. The poor thing was obviously in love with me. And I could see that—well, I had to give him away. That summer we were up in Lake Arrowhead I did it because we were far away."

"The poor thing," Lola sighed, "he loved you."

"See," I said, "so I was *worse* than an animal."

Lola looked at me for a moment and turned away.

"You're sure you aren't just trying to be polite?"

"Me?" I cried.

"That little dog with one blue eye and one brown eye?" she asked. "Why your poor mother!"

"So what else did you do?" I asked, expectantly, longing for anything else she could tell me about being an animal.

"Oh," she said, "there was the time there I was, in the Model T, stopped at a light on Hollywood Boulevard." When suddenly, she was ". . . so overcome, I just *had* to . . ." and she licked her fingers right then and there, shooting her hand up her skirt before the light turned green.

"When I was done, and I was putting it into first gear, just in the very nick of time," she laughed, "I looked up and saw all the people from the streetcar next to me, all watching— they'd seen everything." She laughed now over it all, not turning scarlet with shame in the least which is what I still do whenever things I did like an animal catch up with me —or at least what I did when I imagined no one was looking, finding out I was wrong when it was too late. But I'll probably always be turning scarlet whereas I don't think Lola ever did, even when she looked up and saw the whole streetcar full of faces looking straight down into her lap.

In my day growing up in Southern California meant you didn't grow up, at least not like girls did elsewhere. Having not grown up myself, like Lola, I know what it was exactly —what it is—to be a woman-looking person in your twenties with none of the trials and tribulations bogging down your whole life, driving you from one predictable crisis of adult life to the next until it's too late. I, like Lola, was unable to take adult life seriously in my twenties at all and in fact sometimes I wonder, when I look at adult life even now, how on earth I got myself anywhere past my teens.

Every time the school counselor's office called me down and wanted to know why a girl with my grades wasn't planning on going "on" (i.e., to UCLA), I felt like oatmeal from head to toe.

The idea of doing anything once I got out of the twelfth grade—provided I could even get out since my spelling was impervious to tradition—besides just lying on the beach seemed too much to ask.

"Mother," I once asked, "you don't want me to *become* anything, do you?"

"Only what you really want to be," she said.

"But what if I don't really want to be anything?" I asked.

"I'm sure everything will be just fine," she smiled.

But of course in those days, the early sixties, girls could still get away with "getting married and settling down with some lovely young man," and the school counselor didn't drive me as crazy as she probably would have later. Since looking at Sheena sitting in an office in the Administration Building at Hollywood High, it didn't take a trained L.A. city school expert to realize all I cared about anyway was fun and men and trouble.

Of course there was one thing I wanted to do when I grew up, which I had known all along, and that was to invite people over and have dinner, like my mother.

The thing about L.A. is that there really was no place to sit down. Well, maybe the Stravinskys and people like that had houses where people could come over but most of the people they invited outside of my parents and me all had accents too. It seemed a shame to me that there was no one in all of L.A. who could speak without an accent and be invited over for dinner, and I just knew that there were plenty of people without accents who'd love to come over for dinner and who probably didn't even know what it was like to sit down since they'd spent their lives in L.A. and therefore had no idea how interesting they were.

Already I knew that my best friend in high school—Franny—could talk a perfect blue streak and be every bit as gripping as the people my grandmother always said were brilliant.

And anyway, I didn't necessarily want brilliant people coming over to sit down. I more wanted people who were more or less peculiar, like artists or writers or people Franny and I met hanging around Schwab's who spent their life at Santa Anita going to the races (of course they had accents like people in *Guys and Dolls* which was fine with me). And I wanted people like my friend Ollie from junior high who'd been kicked out of Virgil, L.A.'s toughest *pachuco* high school at that time, and dumped on us at Le Conte where suddenly we had this Japanese girl, Ollie, in the tightest skirt anyone had ever seen, with a razor blade in her hairdo, who sat in the back of Algebra calling it "obnoxious" and getting called down to the principal's office for disturbing the peace. All the people I'd ever met so far in my life who'd struck me as the least bit out-of-the-way I'd managed to keep track of, even when Ollie had been sent to Betsy Ross—the local reform school—and even when she got kicked out of there at the age of sixteen and married a car thief I still always knew where she was. And I wanted all my L.A. people one day to be invited into a large crumbling L.A. mansion (exactly like Franny's which was my dream of a crumbling mansion from the moment she first showed it to me) to eat burritos and drink Rainier Ale and all meet my parents.

And I wanted my parents to invite their friends so the European accents could finally join up with all the other funny bohemians I knew in L.A.—and we could all sit down.

Naturally when I was in the school counselor's office for the yearly question "What do you plan to do when you graduate?" I always stuck to my guns and said, "Oh, I don't know."

"But you've got to be careful that you don't just drift," she'd always say.

"Drifting" sounded fine to me, but to a school counselor it was the Biggest Danger life had to offer.

And that's really all Lola cared about too until she was twenty-six when Vera Minsky discovered her.

THERE WERE PERHAPS a hundred Teretsky dancers during the thirties and forties who passed through the troupe, but of course I only knew four when I was growing up. (My mother and Aunt Helen were not Teretsky dancers and my mother never ever swallowed Trotsky.)

There was Aunt Goldie, Lola, Estelle, and Molly—and of course Goldie was really the star of them all, since Lola and Estelle really only became dancers when it seemed like there was little else to do that was any fun during the Depression. And by the time Molly joined during Lola's last days, nothing on earth could have made her a star like Goldie for she was not foolish enough to put up with notions of such hogwash and, besides, she never could dance worth beans in the first place.

It was at this class that first day that one of the scouts for Teretsky discovered Lola, who looked like a Martha Graham dancer insofar as having black wavy hair (at least before it was hennaed redder and redder). Lola also managed to look like a dancer that day when she was just twenty-six because anything Vera Minsky (the coach) told them to do, Lola could do better than Minsky herself. Or at least longer. Lola never really was driven like Goldie—Goldie *was* a dancer. Lola became a dancer because there was nothing else for an artistic girl bent on adventure to *do* in those days. Lola in fact hadn't even been terribly interested in getting away from her mother—running away from a stifling home. For though Lola's home was probably just as stifling as anyone else's inside, outside it was okay with her.

THE THING ABOUT OPHELIA—my cousin who was Goldie's daughter and when Goldie quit being a dancer once she broke her leg so she married Mad Dog Tim (as I always thought of him), the mild mannered union organizer who insisted on living in Watts to live among the populace and who insisted on working in the factory with the ordinary mortals, so even though he was often up for promotion he never would say yes because he was determined to be as fucked over as anybody till the day he died—was that she was old-fashioned.

And Ophelia—when her mother married Tim and she found herself at the age of twelve moving to Watts—changed her name from Andrea which it had been so far, making herself the character whose youth was sacrificed because some idiot couldn't act nice.

Of course, when Ophelia was twelve she looked ten, and she was another one with black wavy hair and big brown eyes and the look of a Russian wolfhound about her when she laughed. And as she grew into puberty, she didn't look much older because she was always so skinny and so half-crazed-by-anxiety-looking the whole time. Perhaps when she grew up, she might have found herself with a conscience like Lola's and been able to throw herself into picketing, too, except that she'd been raised in the jaws of Mad Dog Tim and had gotten her youth filled up with Socialist Workers' Party kids in camp, meetings, and benefits—and Ophelia wasn't like that.

Whenever Ophelia came over to our house, she took the opportunity to luxuriate.

She luxuriated in the bathtub (because in Watts they only had a shower, even though they lived in a regular house which looked like it ought to have a bath).

In the days when Goldie had danced in New York before she broke her leg, Ophelia had lived there in a flat with cockroaches which made me green with envy. I had no idea until I lived in a flat with cockroaches in New York myself either what a flat was or what a cockroach was, never mind what New York was, and I'd get mad whenever my grandmother got this weepy catch in her throat and said things like "Oi, poor Andrea, she's suffered—how she's suffered!"

Because I always thought, "Suffered! Hah! I don't even know what a cockroach is!"

My grandparents—especially my grandfather, who liked Andrea (even after she became Ophelia) better than either Bonnie or me, probably because Andrea looked like a Russian Jew whereas Bonnie and I looked like goys with a vengeance—were always giving Ophelia things to assuage her for how much she'd suffered and never giving me anything.

Like I remember one time they gave her a set of pastels, an entire set of every color pastel—fifty or sixty at least—that there ever was, plus a huge pad of paper! My grandfather just gave it to her!

"But darling dear," my mother would explain, "that's *all* she's got!"

"That's *all* I want!" I'd insist.

"But Sophie, you have so many things," people would try and make me see when I was nine and Ophelia got the pastels, "you have everything."

"But I want pastels," I'd point out.

I never believed for a moment that having a lovely home, lovely parents, and a cultural background made up for one single pastel and neither did Ophelia—at least not for the first two or three days after Grandpa gave them to her and she gloated around our house where she was staying over Easter vacation, dusting and polishing each separate crayon of chalk before she laid it down in its proper chronological place in the color spectrum. It made me sick.

And then Ophelia herself, after the fourth day—when she finally sighed with ennui over her still lifes and grew as desperately unsympathetic with them and their possibilities as I myself was about my lovely home, family and other advantages—then, but only then, would she sigh tragically over the books in my father's bookcase where so much cultural wealth was in evidence, and say, "Oh, Sophie, how I envy you!"

"Oh yeah?" I said. "Then can I use the pastels?"

"No, no," she gasped, "you'll ruin them!"

"I'll kill you," I shrieked, "I'll call the police! Mother!"

I'd finally complain to my mother.

"She *still* won't let me use them," I said, "and she isn't even drawing anymore."

My mother would look at Andrea and at the pastel box and at me and say, "Why won't you let her use them, Andrea?"

"Because she's not old enough, she'll break them," Andrea said in her well-modulated voice which sounded reasonable to adults. "They're just chalk but I want to keep them perfect because they're all I have. Just chalk!"

"You always get everything and everybody keeps saying it's all you have," I cried. "I wish you were dead!"

"So do I sometimes," Andrea sighed wistfully, moodily all suffering and ready for the next present.

"Well just die then," I urged her, to my mother's dismay.

"Now why don't both you girls go for a nice walk down on the Boulevard?" my mother said. "You've been inside for too long."

The Easter vacation when Andrea was still Andrea and got the pastels, we spent the first few days inside the entire time while Andrea amazed Bonnie and me drawing and smudging with her new pastels, which were so delicate and cloudy like a mist of color drifting over the pages that I drooled with desire to be the one smudging and blending those still lifes together. Every shade in the rainbow came out on paper the way cotton candy did only in pink. Cotton candy somehow in every single blue and all the greens, the reds, the yellows, the purples—even the blacks and browns and in-betweens bloomed into puffy clouds that had only till then been pink. And Andrea refused to let me touch one stick at all.

Bonnie and I were stuck making ourselves do with old broken crayons.

But whenever we actually drove to Watts, to 119th Street where the tract homes lined Andrea's block and they were the only white family anywhere for miles, I realized that pastels were after all only chalk and all Andrea had to live for.

So no wonder whenever she was dropped off to stay with us, she went first to the bookshelves where she trailed her fingertips over the titles which were of novels and plays and art history and all kinds of subjects other than the history of the Russian Revolution by Trotsky or something pertaining to the workers. No wonder she sighed about Salinger and Sartre and Beerbohm and Shaw and Melville and Mark Twain. And no wonder she stood and looked at the drawings my mother hung on the walls, that she herself had done or artist friends or else were reproductions of da Vinci or Picasso or Ernst. And no wonder she would tiptoe into my father's music room when he left so she could look at his collection of Dixieland 78s and feel she was in the presence of the ultimate sophistication.

And no wonder the way she looked at all we had sometimes made me see that it wasn't just broken Crayolas after all. But of course I'd forget when she got a new neon pink Orlon sweater from Ohrbach's which didn't strike me as fair.

Andrea herself, most of the time when we were teenagers or children, seemed to pass through life like a pastel cloud smudged and blended into her surroundings. The quality of her voice became more reasonable too.

"I'm really an orphan," she would explain to me. "My parents were the king and queen and when I grow up, I'm going to become the princess. That's who I really am."

"Really?" I asked, although I believed whatever Andrea told me without question since Andrea never lied and I was only ten.

"That's right," she said.

"Well, I always knew you didn't belong living in Watts," I agreed. "You'd be much more at home in your own castle. On your own throne. With lots and lots of gold and jewels and chocolate cake."

"And my own library," she said.

"Yeah?"

"And lots and lots of jazz musicians," she added, "not just records. To play just for me."

Since having musicians right there playing where I lived was what I grew up with, I preferred chocolate cake. They always let Andrea have all the chocolate cake she wanted, whereas Bonnie and I were stuck because all we had were advantages.

"D ID YOU TAKE THE PIERCE ARROW to rehearsal?" I asked Lola on our walk up Canyon Drive.

"I walked," Lola said. "Right over that hill there. Through the coyotes."

We paused and looked toward Bronson Canyon and west toward the hill Lola had once crossed on foot at dawn. It would have been at least two miles over coyote- and rattle-snake-infested hills till you came down past Valentino's old house to where the Hollywood Bowl was. But to Lola, after so many hikes up Mount Hollywood, these low hills might have seemed nothing in the days when they weren't covered with the houses built on them now.

"On Sunday mornings when your Aunt Goldie spent the night, I'd bring her breakfast in bed," Lola said. "I was so surprised the first time I did this."

"Surprised?"

"Because she'd never had breakfast in bed before," Lola said. "She didn't even know there was such a thing. And I was so unconscious, I just did it without thinking. Because I couldn't conceive of what being poor meant—or even lower middle class. We always had Fraulein to do everything for us before we asked."

"Well," I said, "Goldie sure must know what breakfast in bed is now, thanks to you."

"You know who knew all about being rich? Before anyone had to tell her, she just knew? Goldie's sister, the younger one."

"You mean Aunt Helen?"

"Helen knew everything," Lola nodded. "Just everything. And she sang like an angel. What a voice that gorgeous beauty had, what richness—everything about her just had a glow—golden, that's how she was. And she knew it."

"Before she moved to New Jersey," I said, "and ruined the whole thing."

"These things happen," Lola said philosophically.

"To dumb people, not Helen," I said. "Every time she comes to visit us, you know what she says? She is driving up La Cienega to our house from the airport—you know La Cienega, that hideous street filled with ugly Lowry's Prime Rib restaurants?—and she lets out this musical note sigh like a bell. 'Ooooooo,' she says, 'I'd forgotten how *green* and beautiful L.A. is.' She says that when we're not even any-where green and beautiful yet. She should get a divorce."

"You selfish girl." Lola casually shrugged.

"Well, she should," I insisted.

Lola looked up toward the entrance to the park where Bronson Canyon now lay before us. A thin buzzing mass of sound came twisting from that direction.

"What *is* that?" Lola asked.

"Bagpipes," I said. "A guy practices his bagpipes here because he can't in his apartment, his landlord won't let him. So he practices here."

"Well," Lola said, a birdlike alertness on her intently focused face as she listened for a moment, "he sure does need it."

T HE TOWN WAS SO MISERABLE, even for Texas, that once it had been named "Sour Lake," nobody had the nerve to suggest it be improved. Or the energy. The energy it took to suggest the town at all was about all the miserable place seems to have once known. Attracting tourists by claiming the healthful waters of the sour lake were a cure was the idea behind Sour Lake, but few were attracted and the entire place would have folded, except so much oil was suddenly discovered (which was what had caused the lake to be sour, it turned out) that the wretched town of Sour Lake was still alive.

And Eugenia Crawley was twenty-three years old and still in it—stuck there in Texas, washing the dishes in her mother's restaurant where she waited on tables and was wearing a pink checked outfit, a waitress uniform, she'd made herself. She made all her own clothes on the sewing machine, the kind you pumped—anyway, who needed an electric machine in Sour Lake? There wasn't much reason to sew faster, sewing was all there was to do.

She was engrossed in a serial called *The Girl in the Blue Dress* which the Beaumont paper was running every day. It was about a girl who'd gone to Hollywood from a small town, determined to become an actress and planning to make herself noticeable by wearing only one color, blue. And every day she waited outside the studio for someone to choose her, to notice her, but they never did. Until finally, she was forced to leave her lodgings and wound up sharing a chaste arrangement with a young man who'd also come to Hollywood to make good and whose tiny Hollywood bungalow he let her share, without the slightest trace of anything vulgar. The platonic nature of their arrangement was a simple fact. That the two of them could live in a place where living together at all was possible struck Eugenia as perfect—a place where no small town restrictions, no gossip, could befoul their fun.

She'd tried to survive a year of life by herself in New Orleans where she had lived as a secretary, working in an office. But the office she worked in went broke and the jobs she tried to find were all hopeless. So she'd returned to Sour Lake and was still in it.

Perhaps she was too scared to leave or too loyal to her mother or just didn't know where to go anyway, but once she began *The Girl in the Blue Dress* she found out where to go —Hollywood. Hollywood where you could do whatever you liked. And nobody noticed.

She had her savings and with the help of a Catholic priest from Chicago who was eager to see that anyone who wanted to leave Texas got out even if he couldn't, she even was given a ride—he knew someone driving there who would take her, saving her train fare.

She arrived in Hollywood in 1933 and met Billie, a girl the priest knew who was about her age and also there from the South—only Billie was from Beaumont, a place that was the height of sophistication compared to Sour Lake. Except to Billie, who was one of those people just born knowing they've got to get out of Texas the quickest they can. And since she was so beautiful, Hollywood was obviously her only true home. Hollywood, she felt, was where she belonged.

She felt this even in Hollywood itself where, a year before, she'd arrived and gotten a job as a waitress and a boyfriend who was a waiter in the Coconut Grove. Her boyfriend, like all the waiters in the Coconut Grove, was Italian. He'd begun being a waiter in Switzerland and at the finest hotels he'd apprenticed since he was twelve. By the time he was twenty he was a consummate waiter and his friend, Pietro, also an Italian, was also fully trained. Deciding to come to America—to Hollywood—instead of going to Venice where the hotels needed fully trained Italians from Swiss hotel dining rooms, they arrived first in Canada and then, crossing the border by night, to America, entering the United States illegally and proceeding to Hollywood at once.

Perhaps Rudolph Valentino had been their inspiration. After all, Valentino had been only a poor boy from Italy too. To poor boys from Italy like Pietro and Alphonso, Billie's boyfriend, it almost seemed foolish *not* to go to Hollywood.

Which was why places like the Coconut Grove managed to hire such a finely trained staff—and why a place like Los Angeles, which would hardly seem like the sort of place one would expect to find service so magnificently cosmopolitan, wound up having the kinds of waiters who eventually became maître d's at the world's finest restaurants. New York, in fact, is especially full of maître d's who began in the Coconut Grove as waiters, Italians from Switzerland via Canada by moonlight.

Looking like a hick in her blue dress, Eugenia Crawley carried her suitcase to Billie's front porch and knocked. But she was so shy, adorable, and sweet that Pietro, Alphonso's friend and fellow waiter, fell in love with her at once, in spite of her blue dress.

Hardly giving Eugenia a chance to look for a job, Pietro insisted that Eugenia marry him and not get a job, be his wife instead. She didn't know what to do but say yes. Right off she'd noticed how much like Valentino Pietro looked. His nose was almost exactly identical.

"Yes," she said.

And when they took a weekend off for their honeymoon and went to Laguna, she returned to Hollywood with her hair a new way and a glow of tan and a new dress—also blue —a dress which he chose for her though, which transformed her into a shy beauty and not a pretty hick at all.

In the dance troupe Lola's best friend was the Femme Fatale of the century named Estelle Varez, who wasn't pretty or beautiful or even awake most of the time but really only alive the eight times she managed to get married and divorced. The alimony rolled in.

By the time I met Estelle Varez she was fifty years old and she'd grown as heavy and motionless as the Sphinx. But occasionally she would make up her mind that it was not too much trouble to move. Perhaps consistency demanded that if everything people do was too much trouble, then she had to include doing nothing as too much trouble as well and go make tea. That moment when she rose from her chaise was all I needed to see to know dancing must have rolled off her so obviously that if she even attempted to leap like Goldie the world would end from too broad a gesture. Like that moment with those heaviest boa constrictors when they break out of stony motionless hours or days, suddenly contracting and expanding, making a cataclysmic shambles of their old diamond-shaped skin designs and making mincemeat out of the Physical Properties and Laws of Gravity devised by grave and serious men who insist that everything is dying to fall, to succumb to the earth's pull.

One time, Shelly, one of my deadly earnest girl friends, trying to determine if Estelle was a satisfactory woman up on current events and what was the latest happening to date, found that not only didn't Estelle shop, know about austere films, understand that Hellenic was entirely different and better than Hellenistic styles of art, realize the importance of drugs in the treatment of schizophrenia or the whole new field of psychopharmacology opening up, but after a while my friend finally turned cold when it turned out that Estelle hadn't read *Giovanni's Room.*

"Read?" Estelle laughed. "Why should I bother with such foolishness?"

"You don't read?" Shelly gasped.

"Certainly not," Estelle replied, peeling a grape in her chaise with her long Lincoln Continental Maroon polished fingernails.

"But books are—" Shelly cried, terror impaling her face into Hellenistic horror rather than classical Greek peaceful beauty like Estelle's. "—books are necessary!"

"Necessary? What on earth for?"

"You have to read," Shelly cried, her face stolid as a sleeping boa, "or you can't learn things."

"Why should *I* be expected to *do* anything. Learn things? Read? I think it's very silly of you young people these days to expect people—me—to *do* anything. *Very* silly. And I must say," she must have had to add, "very boring and very tiresome of you—those your age I mean—*do*ing all that. Doing anything is really so bad, but you—your generation —you do *every*thing. It must stop."

"I don't believe you," Shelly now laughed, relieved.

"But it's true," Estelle said, her thumb impaled in a grape which was blacker than her nail polish, thank heavens. If it were green, Shelly might have never gotten out alive. "All of you *do*ing what you'll do. Not only is it silly, boring, and tiresome—it's dangerous, of course, it's bad and dangerous because you don't know *what* you're doing. But dangerous, bad . . . these things are details. Details give women wrinkles. I'm over fifty and I don't have one line on my face. Details! Like good and bad!"

"You're so funny," Shelly decided, consoled that this nice

old lady was only trying to be wicked and witty but didn't know how.

"No I'm not," Estelle replied. Her face settled into a hit-man's closed mask. Not a wrinkle anywhere.

"If I don't go to UCLA I might come up to Berkeley this fall. I'll call you, okay? And come over like this to see you again. . . . I like the older generation you know?"

"How on earth can a grown woman spend the fall in a place like Berkeley?" Estelle demanded of me.

"School," I said. "You know, UC Berkeley? School?"

"Oh, but all fall?" Estelle asked.

"Oh I'm going to be a lawyer one day," Shelly smiled. "And help those more unfortunate than myself."

"And who might that be?" Estelle asked.

"Why the poor," Shelly said, dripping brimfuls of her usual Gamma good intentions—the only sorority at Holly-wood High that never got laid. "We've got to help." Shelly went on, "I mean, we've got to *do* something."

"Darling," Estelle turned to me and said, "I'm terribly sorry but it's just too much trouble for me to get up. And show you out. Can you show yourselves out?"

"Shelly, we're going," I told her.

"Now?" She was in the middle of her first sip of tea and her first cookie.

"*Now!*" I said. "Hurry up."

"That's a good girl," Estelle called out to me as I left, "and slam the door tight, sweetheart. Lock it!"

Fortunately Lola and Estelle formed a friendship origi-nally based on the obvious premise that mascara—Maybel-line black cake mascara you spit into and brushed onto your eyelashes with a caked little brush which fit into the very same little red container—that mascara was the meaning of life. Since they were really the only two in Teretsky's troupe who understood this simple reality, their friendship survived Lola's politics and Estelle's lack of them. And since Lola's radicalism was for The Cause—The Cause being the overthrowing of oppressors known as pigs by the splinter groups, groups Lola and Luther, her black second husband, the present one, were not in now. They were now outsiders from everything because Luther hoped to unite them and attempted to bridge differences and turn splinter groups from hating each other into one large mass of leftists packing clout—Luther was accused of being a tool of the pigs and The Man and got his ceiling filled with bullet holes at lunch. But Lola nevertheless believed the radical ideal that anyone not overthrowing the oppressors was an oppressor by default. And that people who did nothing were going to be sorry after the revolution.

Yet even today I bet Lola's and Estelle's blackened eyelashes and hideous caked little eyelash brushes never ever once rinsed off—they just built until finally, in the end, they were tossed into the trash, forgotten, while a new cake of Maybelline began life, spit and eyelashes were caked blackly, the way Lola and Estelle made sure they were. For Lola and Estelle at seventy still weren't about to settle for one of those new eyelash wands that claimed to make your eyelashes separate and natural and not clotted into bunches and totally unnatural, old-fashioned, and not really nice. But Lola and Estelle at seventy still knew that not really nice, unnaturally blackened eyelashes were good enough for Theda Bara and certainly good enough to steal other women's husbands right out from under them. Other women who didn't wear black mascara and who were confident that the natural look that had blasted its way into being all the rage and forced old-fashioned lipsticks in red and purple to lose their power. And natural flesh tones were unequal to the power they'd gotten from being new. Like natural eyelashes and women who allowed their hair to just go gray without doing something, anything—depending on the natural look to keep their beds filled with men—were blaming men for everything. When Lola's and Estelle's beds were nice and warm. Because their eyelashes were risqué and not nice, just the way men liked them.

Knowledge as primal as Lola's and Estelle's could, I think, have bridged the gap—the deepening gap crevassing between them and all their differences—on the sheer force of the way things really are, which was never ever about men liking gray hair or nature.

It must have been the day I was in San Francisco to see Lola when the woman downstairs with two children who was thirty-two years old came over to tell Lola she'd joined a women's group.

"How sickening," Lola volunteered, looking up from the photo album we were always looking through.

"But we are oppressed," the girl named Joanne said, full of oppressed rage.

"How awful," Lola went on.

"And in our group we are going to learn to have an orgasm. To learn about our own bodies," Joanne marched on further. "To free ourselves from our oppressors."

"That's just awful." Lola's widening eyes comprehended what she'd just heard. "You mean you have never had an orgasm, you're going to a women's group to learn? All of you? On the floor? Like the Hollywood School for Girls."

"Where's that? Hollywood? Well, I went to a Catholic school with nuns and we never even took our clothes all off to bathe. . . . So! It's time to free ourselves from our oppressors. Today was my first group consciousness-raising session."

"Where's Dale?" Lola asked. Joanne's husband was Dale.

"Oh," Joanne said, "he left. He left when he found out I was going to tell people I had never come. He got mad. He said it was a reflection on him. He said if after seven years of marriage I still couldn't come, what was the difference? So he's gone. Now tell me who's the sickening one?"

"You're both just awful," Lola replied instantly. "Just terribly terribly awful. And"—she began to laugh her he-he laugh—"you mean you and a bunch of grown women are just going to lay around and—"

"If you're laughing at me," Joanne said, "you're one of them."

And since Lola couldn't stop laughing even though it meant being one of them, I have the feeling that it must have been that day when learning all of a sudden a new oppressed class had definitely emerged from the masses heretofore unidentified and lacking definition—and it was her. Only she refused to remove her mascara *or* let her hair go gray *or* take off her pancake makeup *or* let people who had only just gotten around to having orgasms tell her that she didn't know about men and women. When it was the only thing she had ever known that hadn't oppressed her—outside of Sam—one bit. Not one.

Maurice Teretsky had a slavish thing about women's feet so overpowering that it was all he could do when he first saw Lola to keep from throwing himself at hers and licking them forever, wrecking her audition.

"Good, very good," he said professionally, not wrecking her audition, "now you will be one of us."

"Oh," Lola said.

"You will come back this afternoon for your first rehearsal. What is your name, *katchka?*"

"Vogel," Lola said, professionally. "Lola Vogel."

"Ahhh," he sighed, "and what size are your feet?"

"My feet?" Lola asked.

Goldie, sitting beside Maurice, tensed into an iron bar of requited suspicions. Her stonelike trance and Lola's raised eyebrows asking "My feet?" made him exercise his tremendous discipline over his reckless urge to lick each of her toes ragged.

"It's her, isn't it?" Goldie demanded.

"You may go," Maurice politely said now to Lola.

Lola made a slight bow and left the stage.

"I knew it was someone," Goldie seethed, "I knew it."

"But my dear child," Maurice said, "I never saw her before today."

"I'll die," Goldie moaned. "Ohhhhhh."

Sitting beside Maurice Teretsky, Lola attempted to breathe lightly and through her mouth. Breathing through her nose when she was around Maurice made her gag, the smell of freshly chewed garlic was so devastating after he ate his breakfast. Trying to offer him Dentyne didn't work because he believed chewing gum was an American abomination, but a week after Lola's induction into the troupe when Maurice had had time to pick a fatal fight with Goldie and clear the decks for someone new, he decided that Lola chewing gum was "charming."

"Except when you are on stage," he explained. "And those are the only two faults in your performance."

"You want me to wear a bra?" Lola asked.

"You must, my dear," Maurice said, "you must."

"But it's so . . . artificial."

"Perhaps," Maurice sighed, "but so is art. And we are artists. We must accept these things."

"I guess." Lola sighed, learning to breathe with her mouth already.

Ever since Lola supplanted Goldie (unbeknownst to Lola until months after she'd been supplanted by Molly), she had become Maurice's little *katchka* (which, she found out, was Yiddish for goose). Sitting next to him during auditions became one of their shared intimacies.

"I didn't mind so much sleeping with him because at five

P.M. he drank a glass of parsley juice and thinned out the garlic, but peee yew I'm telling you, during those auditions —in the mornings—the worst!"

If the mornings were hot during some of those September days, Maurice held his auditions outside and the sky was unnecessarily turquoise, not yet toned down by smog. Every morning now that Lola had become a mistress to her father figure, she got up at the crack of dawn and ran up the trail to the top of Mount Hollywood and then back down again trying to break her own record which she timed on her watch. That she had become a dancer had nothing to do with her determination to keep in shape.

That morning when she got to the top of Mount Hollywood she paused for two minutes to watch the way the sun stretched out in the east and made a clear yellow line on the bottom. L.A.'s horizons could be so flattened sometimes due to nothing in the distance but low hills like Mount Hollywood itself.

There is of course no tree, bush, or flower called Hollywood anyplace on earth, and in fact the only two kinds of things which actually grow indigenous to Hollywood at all are either black oaks or brush, a kind of chaparral which, in September as Lola breathed in the smell, smelled only of dryness about to go up in flames. But at least not of garlic.

Molly had the kind of plump girlish feet with rose-colored little toes that were enough to turn Maurice Teretsky into a slave of burning desire, and he might have thrown himself at these very feet, thus ruining himself and his artistic aspirations forever in "this town" as Hollywood is called, had not those eyebrows of hers (unplucked) saved him and kept him faithful to Lola's feet for almost three more weeks.

Unlike Goldie, who went to bed and thought about suicide, listening to Billie Holiday sing "Strange Fruit" for six days and nights (on a 78), when Lola was supplanted she hardly missed him.

"I mean," she explained, "I had forgotten what a pleasure it was to enjoy one's nose."

Molly van Horn was from that part of Connecticut where Jews weren't allowed to play golf, but she wasn't Jewish and besides she'd never wanted to do anything but dance like Isadora Duncan and planned to dance with Martha Graham.

But the year before Molly ran away to Los Angeles, she had seen the Teretsky troupe and when Goldie leaped out onto the stage like a flying black bird with red lipstick, Molly had suddenly decided she would go west instead in spite of how nobody in her family had gone further west than Philadelphia since before New Amsterdam changed to New York.

And in spite of Edmund Wilson's reports about how shabby and flimsy and fake it all was.

And in spite of the movies.

Because Molly decided that she needn't pay the slightest attention to L.A. or the movies or any other flimsiness—she was sure she could keep a closed mind and not get corrupted.

She was sure she wasn't ever going to go Hollywood, so she went.

IN DOWNTOWN L.A. cafeterias like Clifton's offered all-you-can-eat lunches for a nickel and the Salvation Army had free soup lines for people without nickels at all.

"I was giving your Aunt Goldie breakfast in bed just the way Fraulein did when my sisters and I were little," Lola told me. "Can you imagine? I had never heard Yiddish before. I had no idea what a Jew was. That's how unconscious I was about 1932."

"But I thought you were a Jew," I said.

"I thought so too," she said.

In Lola's house they were such intellectual German Jews with their Fraulein and servants and love of musicales that they didn't even speak Yiddish and Lola had to learn what *katchka* meant in Teretsky's classes along with all the rest of the things she learned about Jews there also.

In my family I would imagine that my father was a Jew because of his black wavy hair but that me, my sister Bonnie or my mother, Eugenia (the girl in the blue dress, who'd actually converted to Judaism in a strange ceremony at the Hollywood Jewish Men's Club where she had to go into the swimming pool dressed in a sheet before a rabbi, and the sheet, she said, "kept floating up around my shoulders, it was not very modest at all"), were Jews—that was impossible. Here I was a blond girl in a leopard-skin bathing suit ready for action in the worst way, drinking Scotch with Claude till 2:00 A.M. contemplating my about-to-be-lost virginity, and my sister with her Bardot figure taking after my grandma in Texas with its boyish derriere and girlish breasts which grew so perfectly, we just couldn't be Jewish. Even my sister Bonnie, who knew what Jews were and who listened when my grandfather told her things, even my sister didn't have black wavy hair and therefore could not be Jewish: her hair was straight and brownish blond like mine and would have been all blond if she'd have bleached it, but she was too nice. Being too nice was why she wound up that summer in New Jersey instead of staying home and learning how to give head from Ophelia like me (not, of course, that she *never* learned to give head).

Of course, my sister always knew more about a lot of things, like being Jewish. She knew how to read music with both hands at the piano (rather than get by learning to play the guitar which was what I did). She knew how to sew from a pattern, how to get straight A's, how to go with the most popular kids in school and get herself elected class president without wearing any makeup or cheapening herself by letting guys feel her up.

But I knew how long to leave peroxide on to keep my hair platinum blond, how to go just to the edge of getting myself pregnant but never quite end up in Tijuana at some abortionist place, how to skip a grade in high school without really doing extra work but simply changing my major so that I had enough credits to graduate half a year early. I knew how to wheedle Lola into staying in Hollywood with me that summer, and I could almost always get the most unconscionable requests of mine granted by some inner instinct for when the time was ripe to ask for the impossible and make it possible in the end after all—at least for me.

I have always believed that life is not fair and that I've been too lucky but there's nothing I could do about it except feel guilty so I do—or at least I try.

That's probably why I always felt so guilty about Claude deflowering me, because I had read many reports that doing it the first time was sure to be a grave disaster but the only thing I didn't like about the first time with Claude was doing it on the rug of my parents' living room with my parents (after they came back from New Jersey) upstairs sleeping in the bed—the nice bed and not the floor.

I expected to lose lots of blood like they did in the Middle Ages but instead I just felt that surely nothing the size of Claude's cock was going to fit in my peculiar case no matter what normal people supposedly did, when suddenly I realized that Claude's cock had been all the way up to the hilt and I still wasn't bleeding.

"Is that all?" I asked.

"*All?*" Claude cried.

"Never mind," I said, trying to be polite.

But finally I knew that I was probably one of those girls who just wasn't meant to have a formal deflowering.

When I told my mother (who had been a trusting saint up till then) she whirled around in a spiral and snapped, "You mean you might be pregnant right now?"

But then we went to a Beverly Hills doctor (one of their friends with the Russian accents) who gave me a diaphragm and I was on my way.

In those days, seventeen-year-old blond girls with tits did not run around looking for trouble with their own diaphragms even in Hollywood—or not every day anyway—but there I was, looking to find someone who could make me feel like I wasn't a virgin once and for all.

I just felt some vital suspension of disbelief was absent—love.

Maybe I somehow knew I was lucky even then because with Claude and his beautiful black wavy hair and the gardenias he left beside my nose on the living room floor (that he'd picked up from Kelbo's before taking me home), all I smelled still was the vicious flower of virginity in the night —and when next I noticed gardenias the night I met Jim, I knew that I finally could never know anything about virginity again.

"You never get enough" was how my mother saw my endless cravings.

"I sometimes do," I'd answer.

"When?" she once asked.

"I can't remember," I once answered.

"See," she said.

It was with Jim, though—it was in those days of wine and opium and roses and noses filled with LSD powder and cocaine—when my ability to consume vast quantities of things that were supposed to poison me from what one rock'n'roll crowd used to call "over boogie" was tested to the hilt and I thought I was invincible.

What they used to call an "iron constitution" was probably why I'm still alive and Jim isn't.

ONE OF THE LITTLE KNOWN FACTS about miserable small towns such as Sour Lake, Texas, which people living in cities like New York or L.A. can't imagine, is that almost nobody ever leaves, not even during a depression, and that many residents like Eugenia Crawley's graduating class from high school stay where they grew up and are quite satisfied with their lot.

The girl in the blue dress who finally married the right man and became my mother in the nick of time was so glad to get herself away from that dustbowl of lost dreams that the very first day she arrived in Hollywood and went to Billie's, Eugenia Crawley found a gardenia bush and pinned a flower to her hair and it became a kind of tacit moment of thankfulness over the rest of her life whenever she pinned real flowers into her hair over the next half century—a kind of thankful prayer for having escaped from the land of oil and onions and her mother's chili dogs and Sour Lake.

If there was ever anyone able to free herself of all traces of a Southern accent, my mother, Eugenia Crawley, did it. Only when she got so mad she forgot even Texas did she suddenly turn out to have the thickest Southern accent on earth.

("Why yo' jus a leel piece of shit onna stick!" she'd suddenly say, out of nowhere.)

Getting married to Pietro two months after she arrived in Hollywood did not dissuade her from finding a job and working. Perhaps it was the influence of her mother's incredible history of marriages over the years, which never lasted or settled anything, which made my mother find the help wanted ads in the newspaper and get herself what her mother always called "a leel jo'. "

("Eugenia, honey, fi' yo'self a leel jo' so you kin be workin' jus in case, you know?" her mother always said.)

Pietro didn't like the idea of a wife who went off to work every morning while he was still asleep, but he felt he could rest easy about the job itself since Eugenia worked as a receptionist/typist in a doctor's office for one of Hollywood's most respected M.D.s. Little did he or even Eugenia know that all hell would break loose five years or so later when the movie star wife the doctor had married was the scandal of the year, caught in a sordid bloodcurdling sex scene with an intellectual from the East Coast who was only in Hollywood for the money anyway and who had not at all counted on people finding out (especially his wife).

The doctor jumped out the ninth-story penthouse window of his office where my mother was the receptionist and went splat on the corner of Hollywood and Highland right across the street from the Hollywood Hotel, where much worse things than those his wife did went on every day and nobody ever jumped out of a thing.

By this time Pietro was the maître d' at a Hollywood nightclub on the Sunset Strip where he worked till dawn trying to get rid of the drunken movie stars and set the tables up for the next night's dinner. And he didn't want Eugenia to work anymore but rather insisted she come with him instead. Since her job hadn't ended too well.

It was at this time that Eugenia and Billie began to see each other again every day. Billie had divorced Alphonso and moved to a little rented cottage on Clark Street just off the Sunset Strip not far from Pietro's nightclub. The little cottage was right down the street from the place where everybody working as a studio musician in Hollywood went to pick up girls, and it was here that my father picked up Billie and made a date to meet her the next day and go have Chinese food for dinner.

Both my mother, Eugenia, and my father, Mort, went to Billie's the next day at five to meet her for dinner (Billie was very mixed up about dinner) and Billie wasn't home. Both of them waited on the front porch and talked for an hour but Billie still wasn't home.

By this time Eugenia was no longer a hick in a blue dress, and she no longer had even a trace of the South in her voice except that she spoke softly (though she did carry a big stick like Roosevelt which no one ever knew until she got mad). She wore her hair parted at one side and curled in honey curls and she wore rayon stockings that were always bagging, running, and having to be mended, and needed endless rearranging with the garter belt buckles before both the seams were straight at once. Rayon, though it was okay for stockings, was not what Eugenia wore otherwise and all her clothes were either pure cotton or pure silk with Mediterranean prints on them like Lartigue photos.

Mort looked like a dark Leslie Howard and dressed in the same kind of casual style which went with his black mustache and the intense blue-blackness of his wavy too-long hair.

No girl stood a chance if she liked that sort of thing and although Eugenia had no idea what a Jew was before she came to Hollywood, by the time she found out it was too late for she was married to an Italian instead.

On their first date they both went their separate ways, he to a Chinese restaurant and she to Barney's for chili where he met her afterwards for coffee and a cigarette. Even he, in those days, smoked like a normal person did back then.

Of course, having spent the last two years of his life trying to recover from the wrong wife he'd divorced before it was too late, when he clapped eyes on Eugenia who was to be the only woman for him ever again, he set about systematically to pry her loose from her Italian until finally he at least was able to get her to have lunch with him in the same restaurant.

"I was already married," my mother says, "what did I want with two husbands?"

The trouble with Pietro was his job. He worked all night and left Eugenia to herself at home finally, not being able to trust drunken movie stars around anyone as beautiful as she was beginning to become—especially after she met my father, Mort.

So Mort had a free hand to convince Eugenia a second husband was the very thing. He found himself a respectable job as a studio musician working for a radio orchestra instead of free-lance, thus providing her with a prospective husband who hardly ever worked past dinnertime. And he found a small little stucco cottage covered with bougainvillea and morning glories with an apricot tree out front and a lawn and she moved in finally and filed for divorce. Pietro did not want to divorce Eugenia but it was too late, she was already pregnant or said she was and by the time she and Mort were married, she was five months pregnant and about to convert to Judaism.

For their honeymoon, they hitchhiked to San Francisco to visit Lola and Sam. Mort had a wonderful time catching up on political and social gossip but Eugenia just thought Jews talked too much and made her sick and she threw up from morning sickness or Jews, either one, all the way home from San Francisco newly married, pregnant, and out of Texas for years.

Going to meet Leah, Mort's mother, whose Jewish heritage made it her solemn duty to keep her children free from *goyim* (non-Jews), especially when it came to marrying them, Eugenia and Mort knew it would not be easy going in there with the pregnancy already showing, the marriage a *fait accompli*, and the two of them so invincibly euphoric. But Eugenia, who was raised by her mother to know that she wasn't trash because trash had no manners and didn't know its ass from a hole in the ground whereas she had perfect manners and upheld this code of her mother's so she was a lady, knew that no lady ever made people feel bad no matter what. So Eugenia carefully chose a bouquet of flowers to bring to her new mother-in-law for their first meeting.

Leah from Kiev, Boyle Heights, and now Hollywood opened the door frowning miserably.

"How do you do," Eugenia smiled, nodding her head in a slight bow as she handed the bouquet to her husband's mother.

"Humph," Leah said, hastily laying the flowers down on a hall table, "better you should bring scissors."

Eugenia and Mort stared at each other. Both were seeing an umbilical cord neatly cut in two with new scissors.

"I am so happy to make your acquaintance," Eugenia nevertheless went on, not stopping a single beat for pondering.

When Mort and Mitzie, Mort's first wife, were married, Leah had hated Mitzie because she had red hair and was a Polish Jew, which was worse than nothing, like a peasant. But when Mort not only married Eugenia but arrived with her radiantly pregnant in a loose, flowered silk blouse and three fresh flowers pinned to her hair, Leah was ready to have nothing to do with any of it and for the rest of her life to wash her hands of Mort like he was dead—though of course he was worse than dead to her.

Knowing his mother, Mort had taken Eugenia to every single family friend and introduced her, letting the softness of her voice and the glow of her skin totally knock them to smithereens. Thus when Leah came to vent her spleen— "How could my Mort marry that *shiksa?*"—to everyone she knew, everyone would say, "But she's wonderful, you are so lucky, I envy you." And everybody did.

By the time Eugenia had to go to the hospital and get it over with and have me, Leah was the envy of all her friends whose children had married nice Jewish husbands or wives and were in the throes of horrors, like Reno, where six-week divorces were simple as pie, which never happened back in Russia when the ghetto and pogroms made divorce a sophistication few could imagine. In Russia, young couples who got married got used to it or else.

Here in America, Leah got used to Eugenia. After all, it wasn't like Eugenia had red hair or anything.

And when I was born nobody could say I had red hair either because I had no hair—just a head. Just a head was all I had for the first eleven months when I just sat around baldly wanting more this and more that, screaming from any room I was left in by myself and supposed to sleep, screaming baldly for louder music and madder milk and hotter entertainments performed live by adults all day and all night.

When it became time for me to go to nursery school I was never old enough and though by then my hair was grown in and covering my bald head, my original bald attitude remained and never left.

Nevertheless, the underlying fact that I was only a baby or only a tiny child later on caused Leah and all sorts of adults in general to ignore my bald head and nature and drool at my skin and fingers and perfect eyelashes like they did for all babies. They wanted to bite babies' cheeks, they wanted to squeeze babies and watch them smile so they could scream with delight. And apparently, even I was able to provide Leah with enough babylike qualities to captivate her and gradually subdue Russia's hold on reality and make California's version seem not so bad after all.

And if I had not been baby enough to soothe the savage beast, then three years later my sister's round little face, surrounded by bright blond curls the moment she hit the delivery room, was.

By the time her second daughter was born and she and Mort were moving into a house in Hollywood where I grew up and where Lola came to stay with me when everybody went to New Jersey, Eugenia had so successfully lost all traces of Sour Lake that only when she was so mad she forgot herself did the girl ever appear as she had that first day on Billie's doorstep—from Texas, the girl in blue.

AUNT HELEN was nearly eight years younger than her brother Mort and only six when she left Brooklyn to take the train to L.A. For Helen, Southern California was not a privilege or a miracle, it was—as it was for Lola—perfectly okay. She was a true L.A. woman from the first week they lived near Hollenbeck Park when she suddenly disappeared and the family, especially her mother, Leah, who went white with irrational shadows of past pogroms in her mind, looked everywhere trying to find her. Finally, there she was, feeding popcorn to the swans under a tree when the rest of them found her. They stood and beheld her as their terror subsided and she said:

"Papa got lost, Mama got lost, brother got lost, and sister got lost," and she smiled and said, "but now they all got found."

Leah raised her eyes toward heaven to silently ask God the meaning of His latest scare when she was stopped by the skimpy tassel-top palm which all over L.A. made light of human suffering in a kind of half-baked attempt at humor.

"*Oi*," she said, and shook her head.

To her, these palm trees were no better than peasants, after this.

She grabbed Helen and knocked the popcorn out of her hand, dragging her daughter to their Hollenbeck Park duplex to teach her what was what before it was too late. But it was too late already, Helen had succumbed to the swans.

"Sophie darling," Helen told me once, "always buy those plums they sell in Beverly Hills. Even though they cost twice as much as anywhere else. Because they are the best."

We were lying in the summer sunshine on the sand. Our striped canvas backrests were side by side and the noises of people and water were appropriate. However, we weren't at a beach or a lake—we were at the Ambassador Hotel, where for a small price people who were not guests of the hotel could mingle with ritzy real rich people.

My father was always taking me and Bonnie, my sister, to this place somewhere out in the valley called Pickwick Pool which—although much larger and more obvious as it was filled with kids, parents, everyone on earth just about—was not the Ambassador Hotel where Helen would take me.

"Sophie darling," Helen asked me once, "does your father have any candy?"

"Yes," I instantly answered.

My father had a wonderful Victorian chest of drawers which particularly fit music scores. When I first knew this chest of drawers existed, I hardly existed myself. In fact, it was taller than I until I became almost twelve. And in it was sheet music neatly divided by composer alphabetically into each of the twenty or thirty drawers, half on one side and half on the other.

However, about three drawers down on the righthand side was a special space with my father's gold medal for violin in it, little packets of gut strings, curiosities from out of Dickens, and although this drawer actually smelled of chocolate my whole life there was never really any chocolate there, there were only peppermint Life Savers.

"You mean your father really has some candy?" Helen asked. "God do I need some."

I was about thirteen and Helen was babysitting for us that night, having come down from San Francisco to scratch our backs. (Helen was the gossamer wings of angel kisses when it came to erotic back rubs for her nieces since we were five.)

I returned with the Life Savers.

"This isn't candy!" Helen burst out.

"It isn't?" I asked. All my life adults had been trying to convince me Life Savers were candy, and although I myself didn't think so and was sure only chocolate was even remotely candy, I had never met an adult until Aunt Helen that day who refused to even look at a Life Saver as though it were candy.

"No," Helen went on, "doesn't your father have any chocolate? I want chocolate. I've got to have chocolate. Where does your mother keep the chocolate?"

"We don't have any chocolate," I meekly confessed.

"You must have some chocolate!"

"But we don't," I said.

"Let's look," Helen decided, "where do they usually keep it?"

"They usually hide it," I said. "But I always find it. And when I do, I eat every last one."

"Oh," Helen said.

"I can't help it," I said. "I love chocolate."

"Let's look anyway," Helen said.

I knew, however, that there wasn't any chocolate in the bottom of my father's socks drawer, the box where my mother kept her chinchilla stole (which, she always said, she got "the hard way—by buying it myself"), the toolbox, the space behind the bookshelf at the foot of the stairs, inside the fireplace, upstairs underneath the paperbacks where I discovered a book by Jean-Paul Sartre called *Intimacy* which was actually so dirty it made me suddenly realize what they meant by orgasm one day when I was twelve, and that orgasms were why adults were so different from normal people was at once abundantly obvious. Suddenly adults became much more complicated than the fools I imagined they were.

Helen and I, however, turned my parents' house upside

down looking for a single M&M but there wasn't one because I had eaten the last one two hours before.

"The only kind of chocolate we have at all is that Mexican."

"*Where!*" Helen suddenly lit up.

In my mother's cooking shelves was always this package of Mexican chocolate which if you chipped it off and went to extravagant lengths to doctor it up in a hot chocolate kind of way still didn't taste worth a red cent.

When Helen ate a chip off it, her face despaired.

"Let's walk to the store and get M&Ms," she said.

"The stores are all closed, it's eight P.M.," I said.

"Ohhhhhhhh." Helen at last nearly wept.

The next morning Helen went back to San Francisco but before she left she confronted Mort, her brother.

"Mort, you ought to have some candy here, what kind of a place is this!" she demanded.

"Aren't there any Life Savers in the—"

"That isn't candy!"

"Well, but—"

"Chocolate, I mean chocolate," Helen demanded. "Sophie darling, this morning before I go back to San Francisco, I'll take you to See's."

"See's!" I cried, See's Candy being L.A.'s most luscious chocolate.

"Yes, darling," she said, looking toward me with a smile. I was a niece after her own heart and not, like my sister, some vapid child with wispy tastes who you'd expect springing from her brother's loins since his tastes were so peppermint too.

("... always buy those plums ... ," she'd said.)

In those days, when I was only thirteen and my parents were both in their early forties, my mother and father had become one of the most gorgeous couples ever established here on earth even in Hollywood.

My father's black wavy hair was getting gray and movie-star-distinguished and he wore tweeds and those loose men's pants they were still wearing—even Elvis Presley himself, during those first few years of Ed Sullivan when he was supposed to be too sexy for the folks to see down past his waist on TV. By this time my father was never without his violin in his left hand and his bow in his right—not *ever*. For in spite of the fact that most studio musicians like him were only required to work a few days a week, my father's obsession with Bach's six violin solos had taken hold never to fall by the wayside like most people's obsessions eventually do. In his determination to play Bach exactly as Bach himself might have expected his music played, my father began altering his Stainer violin (the other very finest make besides Stradivariuses still extant), paring off the improvements added over the centuries by people who couldn't play Beethoven on an instrument with a neck as short as it was in Bach's day for chamber music and a bow outwardly curved so you couldn't hear except in a chamber—and not the Hollywood Bowl. Yet in spite of how obvious it was that if you're going to play Bach, you better start on the instrument he wrote his music for, my father was never accepted at anyplace in America (except Harvard for some reason) because he didn't have a Ph.D. in musicology—even though people who had Ph.D.'s usually didn't play an instrument anyway so how in the hell could they *know* that it made a difference to the music. But in Europe they believed him even though he was a Hollywood studio musician and the research he did at the Bach libraries in Marburg and Tübingen in Germany (which he started in 1932 in Berlin at the library there too) was okay by them. Even if they thought he was crazy at UCLA.

(No wonder I grew up hating that place so much.)

In a photograph in which my mother was over forty, she sits at the outer edge of a gathering of Jewish relatives all huddled in someone's backyard. Three generations of squinting Russian exiles glare into the camera under the noonday sun and everyone is faded, hopeless, listless, and crabby-looking and either they are bulging or they are shrunken, clutching at something. Except that there sits my mother, her face looking away to the side, her neck so swan-like and her face so joyful, girlish, and tenderhearted and her expression so intelligent and gallant, that it's still a mystery to anyone who sees that photograph today how she came to be there.

"Your mother is a saint" is what everybody has told me since I was two.

"Your mother is an exceptional woman, a true angel, a beautiful truly marvelous woman, you are lucky to have a mother like that. Do you know how lucky you are?" they say.

"Yes," they say, "a true saint."

"Your mother . . . ," they sigh.

"Yes," I sigh back.

"What a lucky man he is, your father," they say.

"He is, all right," I say.

"Oh, if only my mother had been like Eugenia," they also say a lot.

"Yeah," I say, knowing what always comes next.

"My mother, boy, now she was a monster! A beast! She used to hold my head under water and try and drown me in the bathtub when nobody was home. Can you imagine your own mother like that, trying to kill you? Your own mother?"

"*My* mother?" I gasp. "All my mother ever did when she got mad—"

"Your mother got mad?"

"All she ever did to me once she started talking in her Southern accent and calling me 'a little piece of shit on a stick' was to—"

"Your mother? What accent?"

"—was to slam me up the side of my head and knock me clear across the room just like she said she would—once all of a sudden Sour Lake, Texas, came into things like 'Ah'm gonna slam yew cleah 'cross thees heah room, kid, ri' up the side yo head, now you heah?' " I'd mimic, "and before I could duck, there I'd be. Clear across the room landing against the wall."

"The wall?" they'd ask. "Your mother?"

"With my mother if she knocked someone, the only way you were ever about to stop just about was if you got to a wall."

"Your mother?"

"Of course, she would never do it unless she was sure you'd land against a wall. I mean, after all she is a saint you know."

"After all . . ."

The only thing I've ever come across in nature that captured her spirit or did her the least justice, almost the way Giotto portrayed St. Francis and showed us the way to understand the whole picture, was when I was reading this book on snakes and discovered one called the black mamba. The black mamba, unlike my mother, lives in the West Indies. However, he whirls on his victim, chasing an entire horse going sixty miles an hour for just one bite. One bite from a black mamba can drop a horse dead in his tracks, the snake's venom is so deadly no grace period is allowed for heroic actions by men of destiny. The picture proposed by my brief brush with the awful image of a snake that goes sixty miles an hour to fell a horse made me nostalgic suddenly for the way my mother used to whirl into foul words in Southern hisses which warn too late of what is to happen once the perfect saint in all divine grace and beauty decided to knock me clear across a room like she said she would before I could escape, landing me against the far wall with one bite of her hand, felled by my mysteriously perfect mother who, unlike the black mamba who is of the Elapidae family which includes the cobra, lived in L.A.

M Y SISTER AND I began referring to our parents as Them the year we went to Paris and they went to Germany when we were actually separated from Them months on end.

The passion my father had been born into by growing up practicing violin in order to win the gold medal away from Lola had been broadened in Europe, where for two years he studied with a real master. In those two years he wised up, knew who the newest composers were, learned to play Stravinsky and what atonal music was supposed to be. The time we were in Paris was when they were hoping to see Sam Glanzrock (where he made his last two films on a Guggenheim grant) and missed him by one day in fact.

In the pictures Sam took of them on their honeymoon, they had hitchhiked up to San Francisco and were staying with Sam and Lola in Haight-Ashbury before the fall. In the photograph my mother looks like she's about to throw up and my father with his wavy black hair and mustache looks perfectly demure now that he has wrested my mother from her marriage to Pietro.

He is sitting demurely with his hand on her knee. Her knee is encased in a rayon stocking. The stocking is held up by a garter belt but the garter belt is kept together by a large safety pin. Like all her clothes, it is too small and her waist just way too large because now she is five months pregnant,

63

one week married, eight days divorced, and all she wants to do is just throw up.

My father wore clothes like one of those English movie stars with mustaches and voices like rose petals, though my father's mustache made his look much handsomer than theirs. His voice was more like nasturtium petals, some petals that grew only where it was always a little too hot. My father's passions for Trotsky, the violin, and my mother were always a little too hot, too.

For my sister and me after Paris, they were always whom we meant by Them.

THE FIRST MOVIE I saw was *Bambi* and naturally I had to be removed from the theater before fifteen minutes had gone by since I was already so white with fear I hiccupped instead of wept and I couldn't even scream—the images on the screen drove me so crazy. But somehow later on, my sister and I managed to see musicals, although the first one I remember called *Cover Girl* with Rita Hayworth I couldn't stand except for looking at her face and the noise was so loud that finally when we got out I had to throw up, my inner ear was so gonged up. But when once again my parents attempted to see if we could make it through a Walt Disney family classic and Bonnie and I were ushered by both my mother and father into *Fantasia* with one of them on either side of us in case we had our usual nervous breakdowns, neither of us blinked, we were so utterly spellbound by the majesty of the sexy giant bat whose wings seemed to be made out of volcano eruptions.

Only of course when we tried to sleep that night we both woke up crazy with horrible terrible sexy volcano dreams and for two whole weeks we both woke up screaming so badly that finally my father, who'd been in Freudian analysis fashionably early and thus knew all about everything, took us one morning into his study and showed us (my sister was seven and I was ten): one cardboard box about a foot and a half square, one can of black enamel paint, one paint brush, one newspaper, and one roll of rubber bands—oh, and some scissors and some construction paper in pink and yellow.

"Now," he began, "I want you both to watch quietly."

First he painted the box black (it must have been fast-drying paint—maybe it was India ink, not enamel). Then he cut out two triangles in the top of the box parallel to each other and about an inch or so apart. Then he cut a pink oval out of the construction paper and pasted it firmly below the triangles. Then he cut a yellow triangle out of the yellow paper and pasted it between the two first shapes.

"Now," he said, "here, you hold these."

He carefully rolled up two wands of newspaper and secured them with rubber bands, handing one to each of us. Then he stuck the box on his head and got down before us on his hands and knees. Then he said, "Now hit me."

Bonnie and I were a hopeless shambles of embarrassment.

"Go ahead," he said, "you know—like I'm the monster. From your dream. Hit *it*."

My sister began laughing hysterically.

"*Now* what are you *doing*," my father cried, annoyed, and he took off his head and led us out to the backyard where we had to stand in the Australian grass in our bare feet all day, he said, until we hit him—or he wouldn't let us go play.

Finally, daintily, and both at once, we pretended to slap him with our wands.

"Harder," he said, "to make the monster go away."

So we pretended he was the monster, hit him harder with the harmless newspaper, and that night we slept clear through totally cured.

He was positive his technique had worked.

But I was positive we were just doing it to be polite. After all, another vision of our father out in the crabgrass on all fours in the backyard was enough to keep your screams to yourself.

THE ONLY TIME I remember seeing Sam Glanzrock was the time in about 1952 or so when he and Aunt Helen drove down from San Francisco high on peyote all night and showed up at our front door the next morning fried out of their minds, Aunt Helen laughing her virgin-spring laugh and Sam darkly creating a cloud in my memory which is all that I can recall today—for what was most important about meeting Sam that day was that I realized how much he loathed children, especially me.

Sam was out in the front yard where my father had dragged out one of the living room armchairs so they could drape this black velvet coat of my mother's over it, which would be used as a backdrop when Sam took a photograph of my father's left hand holding the neck of his restored eighteenth-century violin—which wouldn't have worked at all if the swing in our front yard were used as a background, even I as a child by then could understand—and the sight of two grown men that day who looked to me as though they were playing house with a chair in the yard, and the intensity with which they both stood back to look at the way the velvet fabric would drape, was too miraculous for most children, especially me, to stay inside.

As far as I was concerned, no man ever made me forget he was a shrimp any faster than Sam (except Stravinsky, of course, but then Stravinsky always made everyone else seem bloated). Just from meeting him once, when I was that young, I was so determined to overcome his hatred of me that all I remember feeling is that I'd do anything to be a woman enough for him, like it was my job or something to grow up and try and soothe his savage eyes. Whatever color they were.

Everyone who knew him said they were a different color. My father insisted on gray.

"Yes, but he was so fascinating," Goldie said, "he *looked* so hot. That dark skin, those lavender eyes!"

"Lavender?" I cried. "Daddy says gray."

"Your father didn't know anything!" Goldie sighed, about her own brother.

"Anything?" I cried.

"Well, Mort was a good musician and everybody was a little afraid of him because he was so smart and sarcastic," she recalled, "but after he came back from Nevada, he was a lot better."

"Nevada?"

"To stay with your mother before she got divorced," Goldie said.

"My parents went to Reno together?" I asked. "Is that legal?"

"Didn't anyone ever tell you that?" Goldie asked.

"Why didn't Sam ever pounce on you?" I said. "I mean he pounced on everyone, didn't he?"

"I never knew," Goldie said. "You know, it worried me. I asked Helen to see if she could find out when she lived with him, so one day she asked him."

"She did?"

"And you know what he said?" Goldie said. "He said, 'Oh, I couldn't do that to Goldie!'"

"That bastard!" I cried, comfortingly, since Goldie looked very depressed, and then, trying to think of something to cheer her up, I added, "He meant you were too good for him, you were too great an artist, you know? After all, when he first met you, hadn't you just come back from New York where they said you were so great?"

67

"Maybe that was it," Goldie agreed, looking relieved, "I
was too good for him, wasn't I?"

"Reno? My parents?" I sighed.

"You know," Goldie said, "I introduced Lola to Sam."

"No kidding," I said. "What was she like?"

"She had a great body," Goldie said, "and she didn't mind
showing it."

It must have been in 1939 or so, the year Lola met Sam,
when she had been in the dance troupe about two years, and
had been living in New York (where the troupe went that
year) with an especially cute dress manufacturer who was
German (and probably spoke German to Lola) who Lola always called "the bigshot" (and Goldie always called "the
Fascist"). (Goldie and Lola lived in the same cold-water flat
in New York where Ophelia remembers nothing except
cockroaches.)

Lola took the train to Hollywood again, because the summers and winters on the East Coast were not what she meant
by those words. She was almost twenty-eight and she had so
far indulged herself almost entirely in wrestlers, Hindus,
and bigshots. Whenever I asked her why she gave Sam the
time of day, she always said, "He was a genius, you know,
everybody said so."

"A genius at what?" I wondered.

"Photographs."

Sam spent the thirties living on twenty-three dollars a
week that the WPA gave artists and photographers during
the Depression, and in Santa Monica where he lived this
was enough to afford to live in a bungalow court on Strand,
a few blocks from the beach. In fact, during the Depression
in Santa Monica, a lady who lived there told me you could
get a house with a living room, four bedrooms, a kitchen, a
breakfast room, three bathrooms, a dining room, a sewing
room, a front yard and a backyard for forty dollars a month
(the guy who taught dance then was Marge Champion's fa-

ther in Santa Monica, he had a studio, the lady who told me said, where she took lessons as a child).

Goldie, the only one he didn't do in (besides my mother), seemed to be the only one who ever knew what Sam actually was like, for she's the one who said, "He always dressed better than any of the other guys. They were all a bunch of bums. Not your father, but all the others."

"It was just after I'd come back from New York where we were dancing that summer," Lola said, "and I had nothing to do with myself, so I went to a movie, by myself, on Hollywood Boulevard—I should remember the movie, but I can't—it was with that one who steals clothes."

"Oh, you mean, Hedy . . . ," I said.

". . . yes, and the usher in back of me kept saying 'now it's going to get good, now it's going to get good . . .' "

"Did it?"

"No," she said, "when I got out, there was still nothing to do except I ran into Goldie, who was going over to this fellow's house who had a marvelous record collection, where your father and Sam and that friend of theirs—God, I can't remember his name either—anyway," Lola said, "we went to the house of this record collector, and that was when I met Sam. He and the other two fellows were almost fighting to take me home."

"But why did you pick Sam?" I asked.

"Because he was a genius," she said.

"But everybody in those days was a genius," I said.

"But Sam loved my feet," Lola added.

"Oh," I said. "Knew how to show a girl a good time, right?"

"But I didn't love him," she insisted, "we were just living together, but Mother asked me one day when she was going to see the announcement of our marriage in the paper. We had the nicest house, too, overlooking the Hollywood Bowl —we could hear the concerts."

"You did? I thought Sam lived in Santa Monica," I said.

"Hein bought us a house," she said.

"Oh," I said.

"I had to get married, or Hein never would have sailed to Honolulu on the *Luralai* the next week," she said.

"Oh," I said.

"And I had nothing else to do," she went on. "I guess I used Sam because he was so mad about me, and I was lonely." And she looked guilty, adding, "Besides, the man I left in New York—not the bigshot, but another dancer who I was with the time I toured when Sam and I were together and he stayed home—was interesting in bed, but no place else. And you know Sam had those eyes of course. . . ."

"And Sam was terrific in bed too, right?" I said.

"Sam? I should say not," Lola indignantly protested. "There were three or four lovers in my life who *really* understood what they were doing—but Sam, my heavens! No! But he did have a nice little body, except for his lower legs."

"His lower legs?"

"From his calves down, but above that, he really looked like a naked prince on a horse in a Maxfield Parrish print. In fact, your Aunt Helen had the same print in her bedroom. The same one! So I knew I was right, because why would she hang it up if it didn't look like Sam."

"Oh," I said.

When I asked Lola what color Sam's eyes were, she said, "It wasn't only his eyes, it was his eyebrows—they went straight across the bridge of his nose. They made him look terribly . . . terribly . . . I don't know . . . exotic."

My mother, when I asked her, said, "Well he had that look, you know, green eyes, but he was myopic like your father. They both had that look."

"How come you didn't get impaled by Sam?" I asked. "Or did you just meet him on your honeymoon?"

"Well, for one thing, I was in love with the best one—your

father," she said, "he was just as salty, but he had more class. Besides, he wore a tuxedo."

"Oh," I said. "By the way, what was Daddy doing with you in Reno?"

"It's none of your business," she said.

When Lola first went to live in San Francisco with Sam, she married into a time and place which had nothing to do with her. It was WWII and she had to completely abstain from speaking German—any German at all—since the whole country including herself couldn't hear it without boiling over, and though she was used to occasionally dropping German flourishes into her everyday speech, she no longer dared even for fun. Plus, in San Francisco, a woman from L.A. had to resign herself to hats and gloves and stockings because no woman could go out wearing a belly dancer outfit for fun. Women were respectable.

Perhaps the real reason Lola married Sam wasn't to be polite or to oblige her mother, but really because she thought she ought to do something that wasn't fun—to strengthen her character—something womanly like sacrificing her life. But then I still couldn't see why anyone would marry Sam just to get character.

"Everything had been just fine until the first week we went up there," Lola explained. "The first week we were married I got sick. I had a temperature of 103 degrees and *he* was very proud of me, by the way, the first day or week—*he* anyway went out, that day when I was sick, to a party. A big party!"

"Oh?"

"And before he went out, two girls from the class he taught came to pick him up and take him, and I said, 'Well, what do I do while you're gone?'

"And he said, 'Anything you wish.'

"And you know, what? He left his new bride."

It sounded to me like a case of misunderstanding. Lola misunderstood Sam, thinking he ought to have stayed home with his new bride (*her!*—everybody always thinks in terms of mythic figures when they're involved: "the new bride," "the faithful lover"), and Sam misunderstood Lola, figuring that since she'd never cared that much before and had always taken off for New York on a passing dance whim that surely now that he was in his first glory—his first professional employment that wasn't WPA-funded or in a plastics factory like my father and all their friends for the War Effort —she would realize that he was just taking off on a passing party whim.

It's funny how when people get married, they suddenly get mythic about love. Even when they don't care about who the myth is starring.

T HE SUMMER THE CRAVENS MOVED IN, I was only five but I still remember feeling outraged that anyone as beautiful as Molly Craven could have been was absolutely determined not to do it. There she was with the most perfect smile and this nice wavy light brown hair and a pretty figure (which, according to Lola, had been even prettier when they danced together in Teretsky's troupe for the short time Molly, who was once Molly van Horn, put up with all that feet arousal stuff) and she utterly refused to wear lipstick, let her hair fall down to her shoulders, or put on a dress any color but gray.

Until years later when I found out what Connecticut was and who preppies were, which suddenly made so many things clear to me (like *The New Yorker* and people on the East Coast who weren't Jewish), Molly seemed to me totally devoid of taste. All the quaint New Englandy wallpaper, her preoccupation with Shelly's schoolwork (when everyone else in L.A. merely hoped their daughters wouldn't get too done in by the movie business), and her inability to stand anything glamorous, including chocolate, seemed at the time to be the result of no taste at all, and not—as I saw afterward —of a definite object in mind for how things should be.

I guess when she left Teretsky (after he went ape when she refused to wear toenail polish), she only stayed in Hollywood because she met someone who was even more of a Yale product than her brothers—Mitchell, for even though Mitchell was already getting small parts in movies and was an actor, his roles were in such good taste it was hard to remember he was in Hollywood at all and hardly anyone went to see him.

When we were children, all Molly ever tried to do was organize everything, and all I ever tried to do was disorganize them. The thing was, my mother let me and Bonnie stay out past sunset in our bare feet wearing underpants during the summer (and nothing else), roaming around anywhere we wanted to, whereas Molly had her timetables and schedules planned for Shelly and her brother Toby every minute of every decade. And so when a friend of my father's died and left a treasure chest of pipecleaners and glitter (which he had used to make figurines of musicians playing instruments) and I used it to make an underwater peepshow with mermaids using blue cellophane for the sky, Molly was so incensed she sent me home, saying, "Your mother lets you do anything you want," and added, "no wonder you're too creative!"

(Every time Bonnie or I made a peepshow, Shelly and Toby got another bike.)

To me, growing up and watching Molly shove back every lock of hair which dared to fall across her brow and come home with more gray outfits and never go to San Francisco for summer vacation—just Yosemite—the refusal perpetually in her soul to acknowledge the goodness of beauty was a ghastly crime. A crime, though, which I felt somehow I could alleviate in her, so year after year I tried. But no peep-show, no mermaid, nothing ever convinced the Cravens to let L.A. into their hearts.

When I was only five though, I thought Shelly's mother was simply no good because she was somebody else's mother, I suppose, and not mine. But after that I began hating the lady who was to look with haughty preoccupation on almost every good idea I came up with in my entire childhood. The competition between her daughter and me might have really been insane except that I was half a semester behind Shelly because I was a few months younger and besides, I was no good at anything.

I was unable to read school books, just bumbled through, while Shelly if she couldn't get an A in something had to have a tutor like the ignoramuses and morons who got F's always did. I got special permission by the second grade to be allowed to leave the school grounds and go home for lunch because we lived within a couple of blocks, but Shelly, who lived nearer than I did, was forced to stay with the mad scramble throughout lunch "facing reality" her mother called it. So it was no wonder when I somehow also managed by the fourth grade to go home for "nutrition," which nobody had ever gotten to do before, that when Shelly turned green with envy till she caved into hysterical sobs her mother would naturally wish I were dead. Or deader.

The idea that school was anything but an unnecessary evil that a child should be encouraged and abetted to get out of was my mother's specialty.

"What do they know, they're only the teacher" was my mother's usual instinct about the entire place.

Naturally not even the wife of a radical Stalinist, like Shelly's mother, could go along with my mother and it was lucky my mother was a saint or she might have driven normal mothers crazy.

The trouble with Shelly's mother, I suppose, was that she was a person who believed in ideas like they were any good at all and like you could instill a sense of discipline and good posture and an ability to concentrate when such things were not worth instilling unless you lived on the East Coast or someplace so awful a person might need to sit up straight.

All year long Molly would bustle around as though a long hard winter were coming to kill us, and it didn't do any good to wish she would stop her brimming *idées fixes* and take a look at the weather surrounding her all over the actual landscape because she was too disciplined and concentrated to ever believe that you could face reality and hardly notice anything awful about it at all.

She was such a miracle of consistency that she even drove my mother crazy sometimes wishing she were just dead so she could forget the whole business.

Every day she primly parted her light brown hair in the middle and braided it in the back and knotted it up so it didn't distract anybody from reality. Then she washed her face in Ivory soap which I'm sure she secretly wished were really pure and not just 99 and 44/100 percent, but she probably had to make do. Then she found the most obscure dress in her closet which was as clean as a nun's hat but a lot more modest and she put it on so it covered her arms and knees and collarbones. Everything she owned zipped in the back. Buttons down the front were too suggestive. She never shaved her legs or wore heels, and in black ballet slippers she took Shelly from ballet class to cello lesson to her tutor or her private specialist in posture exercise.

The sky still hangs overhead filled with smog which nothing Molly ever did could expel from the listless days of summer which are as listless today as they were when Shelly and I took swimming class three times a week at Hollywood High. (Hollywood High today is even worse than it was all along. The trouble with Hollywood High today in fact is that the pimps across the street south of Sunset at Highland tie up traffic so completely that at three when school lets out you can hardly budge an inch.) We were only ten years old when we'd come from an indoor pool with eyes inflamed from chlorine and be blinded by burning smog, enough to force us to just go straight home practically and not go to Brown's "Home of the Hot Fudge Sundae" and get a hot fudge sundae, but we always made it to Brown's and managed to sit down and order in time to have a last dying meal.

What I really liked to do, unless a layer of smog covered the sidewalk so badly that you had to go straight home on the bus or die, was to dawdle along Hollywood Boulevard and walk the entire mile or so home. The hotter it was, the better I liked it although if it rained I liked it too.

Naturally Shelly was too sensible and never dawdled away her busy childhood summers on Hollywood Boulevard and even with the crowd that day in front of Grauman's Chinese, which was on her way to the bus stop and therefore not dawdling, she would have gone right by and missed everything if it hadn't been for me.

But fortunately I was not the type to miss Marilyn Monroe and Jane Russell.

There they were, both of them.

"It's Marilyn Monroe," I trembled.

"Don't grab me so hard," Shelly screamed.

"Look at the cement and everything right there," I said dying.

"And Jane Russell with the same dress on," Shelly sighed, "both dressed alike."

The dress was white with black polka dots and the neckline plunged daringly, the bust was fitted, their tiny waists were zipped up the back and the skirts were full and yards and yards of black polka dots hung on the white background down to their knees. Photographers were everywhere trying to make Marilyn look at them and Jane Russell looked bored. And Jane Russell's nose was scary close up. This was just when Monroe had become a star in *Gentlemen Prefer Blondes* but I had already seen her in *River of No Return* nine times and I had a record of her singing "River of No Return" and now she was just right here in the smog before me.

We emerged from the crowd a half an hour later having watched both her feet in high heels and both her hands cemented. You were able to stare into her cleavage while she smiled. Bombs bursting in air couldn't have been more like American poetry.

Shelly and I were too exhausted to speak. I had to take the bus home I was so drained.

We walked up our street under the chartreuse leaves of the trees and one by one passed the lawns before the one in front of Shelly's house and everything was quiet and silent, likable but not right of course with Molly standing there ominously.

"You are never to make my daughter late again," Molly said. "From now on I'm picking Shelly up from school and if you wish to get a ride home too then very well but I'm not letting Shelly do anything she wants like you, is that clear, Sophie?"

"I didn't make her late," I said.

"We saw Marilyn Monroe," Shelly said.

"Another one of those stories," Molly deduced, yanking her child inside where she could decompress from smog among other bad influences. But, after all, I preferred dawdling down Hollywood Boulevard by myself to going straight home after swimming sensibly and since I wasn't the one who learned the cello or stood up straight while L.A. stayed the same and Hollywood High got worse, I was prepared.

Walking home down Hollywood Boulevard past streets

like Cherokee I was already pretty sure Hollywood was doomed long before the smog first killed off all the pepper trees lining the streets north of Hollywood Boulevard, which had created rosy clouds overhead before the smog, but after the smog, well. . . . People in their thirties would shake their heads and sigh, remembering how beautiful things had been before they went downhill.

People in L.A. just had no real sense of what a true city was, but since I was not prepared for a true city it was hard to imagine what people with real sense were like. Unless they were all like Molly.

The funny thing was that if anything had ever happened to me I know Molly would have flown to the rescue without a second thought—but luckily she never had to save my life, otherwise I'd never have forgiven her.

EVERY NOW AND THEN my mother and father simultaneously seemed to have a tacit understanding that struck both of them like a bolt from the blue and all of a sudden they would have a party and would instantly telephone the people they were going to invite, and before anybody knew what hit them my mother had amassed so much food that if you opened the icebox the house would collapse because first the tamales tilted over and smashed headlong into the whole slipshod game plan laid out on the kitchen table piled up with too many pots and too many stacks of damp paper wrappings to keep the handmade tortillas fresh in a package of a dozen each, and of course too many tomatoes were toppling around onto whole onions lying all over everything and then packages of jack cheese kind of lay there in rectangles thrown down any which way like meaningless books, and a bulb of garlic would roll out from under the cans of chili my mother used for *rellenos* because we decided that chili *rellenos* were actually better made from canned chilies because fresh ones were intractable and too hard like rock on one end and canned ones were divine, *diviner,* but once the cans began rolling off the table onto the floor and all the large soup pans came down if they got knocked over by the tamales because someone had tried to open the icebox, then no wonder our entire house would simply end in collapse along with all hopes and dreams glutonously shaping up for the party, which was why everybody stayed out of the kitchen and left my mother alone to contend with the icebox door since it was her party and all her parties were struck by the same bolt streaking through the tacit understanding from the beginning to the impossible-for-anything-to-go-wrong ending.

But of course it was impossible for anything to go right about my mother's crammed parties because when we moved into the house in Hollywood when I was five, the little dining room just right for four people perhaps had been relentlessly wallpapered with gigantic roses in overblown pink which were woven in a trellis of gray all enlivened by green leaves much too large like the roses which were five or six inches across. The pink petals flopped like they were swooning over true romance and nobody but my mother would have allowed that wallpaper to remain in her home defiling her walls and being in such questionable taste that maybe she herself might be from Texas after all, maybe people in fact looking at that wallpaper would become unsure my mother was really a saint and perhaps she was simply an impossible person like Elmer Gantry passing herself off as an innocent dainty miracle but really just a vulgar *shiksa* like my grandmother had deduced all along, a nobody who'd just used her feminine wiles to catch the sensitive genius my father was believed to embody in those circles because nobody could get to first base with him, the girls died for him, he never even threw them down on their backs carelessly and used them for his own lust like men did in those days when they only wanted one thing and my father was not even willing to endure their company long enough to get the one thing and then wish he hadn't. Not like Sam Glanzrock.

"I came," Sam Glanzrock used to announce, "where's my shirt?"

"You mean, 'I came, where's my shirt?' was what he actually told them?" I asked Lola.

"It was his eyes," Lola remembered, "his eyes were that gray. That gray he could say anything and look at you and you quick ran and got him his shirt."

"What color gray does that?" I asked.

"All I remember," Lola said, "is that *that* gray in his eyes was why you'd get him his shirt."

"But gray . . . ," I dubiously grumbled.

"But *that* gray," Lola explained so I'd never forget. "Don't think you know everything because you're from Hollywood. After all you're only eighteen."

(I was seventeen, but it didn't matter, I was from Hollywood and I was positive I knew everything and gray eyes were not included in what I knew.)

Half the girls seemed to want my father to give them a tumble and then drop them so they could experience that pain of life like Anna Karenina, though he probably was too conceited to slum around riffraff *hoi polloi* he probably thought dancers were, while the other half decided any genius so sensitive simply could not dally with just anybody unless it was true love because after all he was a violinist and a man who played the violin was simply inviolate with sensitivity and no woman on earth was probably good enough for such a dashing tormented figure.

Only suddenly walking down the street one day my Aunt Helen told me, "There was Eugenia, dressed like a flapper, you know, the cutest thing with those little feet she had, her dress was silk and it had flowers all over it and she was wearing real flowers right in her hair—real ones. . . . Oh, I didn't think my dumb brother had sense enough to ever find a . . . a daffodil like your mother but your mother didn't seem to mind him, you know? And she was smart too. And she *still* didn't mind him. And she was wearing yellow shoes. Yellow! Ohhhhh, with little heels, what an adorable darling thing she was."

I could imagine her flapping down the street, her flapper look seemed to have flared on into the thirties in spite of the Depression and everybody else being so depressed they dressed depressed. Her curly hair was dark blond in those days and her lipstick was Tangee orange.

In those days she turned out pies by the cloudful, bringing forth enormous lemon meringue specials for my father to indulge in because when you're Jewish among Jews nobody gives you any pies, especially not lemon meringue, and nobody ever pulled pies out of heaven like my mother did when she was still the best baker on earth, but that was before she encountered Molly and Mitchell Craven, over for dinner the first time, when all my mother made was mere hamburgers and they were such hamburgers from above that Mitchell Craven loudly remarked, "Molly, why don't you make food like this?"

My mother never allowed cookbooks or directions to interfere with her impossible dinner parties, stuffing people into that claustrophobic mash of impending roses and ladening the table with more tamales on top of more tacos next to the *rellenos* and their sauce and everybody was all pink and florid as the roses and laughing insanely because more food just kept being brought forth and nobody could eat one more bite only they did and everybody was ready to be rolled home by dessert which was an Italian Giocino's cake, a rum cake covered in flowers. We had coffee so strong it enabled people to actually rise from the table and manage to unravel themselves out of the space in order to go play Bach quartets, drunkenly smoking cigars and laughing their heads off until it was 11:30 and everybody had to go home until the next bolt.

My mother's parties never dropped a stitch and nobody came away wondering what on earth all that rose-petal wallpaper meant. Instead they believed it was what it really was which happened to be gorgeous and as perfect as possible struck like a bolt from the blue forever into their memories.

The summer Mitchell Craven got blacklisted and Shelly and I who were only in the third grade and used to walk home from school past the lawns on our block, one by one, beneath the chartreuse trees in June, was the summer the Cravens, not us, got to finally get a TV. But only to watch the people being blacklisted throughout the McCarthy hearings, not to watch Perry Mason which would have been why I would have wanted to have a TV.

"Maybe Daddy'll never work again," Shelly used to laugh, bravely (like her mother), "and we'll have to go to the Poor House. And nobody will come visit us."

"Oh," I said, "I'll come visit you every day."

"Maybe the Poor House is too far away," Shelly complained.

"My mother will drive me," I said.

"Yeah," Shelly brightened, "and she could bring us tuna sandwiches, okay? My mother's are always the lowest. I wish we could just get my mother to disappear and only have your mother."

"Why don't you poison her?" I suggested.

"Yeah," Shelly said, "but what would we poison her with?"

"Iodine," I said.

"Okay," Shelly said thoughtfully.

But we forgot.

As if being blacklisted wasn't enough, terrorizing Shelly into two years of the walks to school being occasionally spiked with visions of a Poor House somewhere out on the edge of L.A. where we'd bring her a tuna sandwich, then actual figments of Lillian Hellman's imagination materialized and began making phone calls to Molly calling her a dirty Commie and anonymously threatening her with scary phone calls from honest real Americans who were proud of their country and therefore if she came and showed her face at the PTA meeting the next Friday, she'd get what she deserved and they were just warning her not to come, for "The PTA don't allow no reds."

"Ooooooo," Molly cried, dropping the receiver like a horrible surprise of death.

"Oh," she said to my mother running as fast as she could across the street before they could catch her or trap her alone in her house, "I'm afraid to go anywhere, now I'll never go to another PTA not ever, oh, I'm so afraid what shall I do, oooooo. . . ."

Luckily Molly was so wracked dry with fear and hiccups and sobbing that she didn't notice what I noticed, which was my mother leaving her halo in a shell of hollowness while she snapped into a fully realized raging snake which she snapped right back out of, thank God, and was relighting up her almost perpetual glow before Molly saw it and knew that it couldn't have happened therefore she must be crazy and she'd have a nervous breakdown to match.

"Now listen honey dear," my mother began, calling her the soothing things she called me to fix my nightmares at night or my screams in the daytime from penicillin shots mainly, and if anyone ever needed fixing and being called honey dear it was Molly. My mother's hand stroking Molly's neat head calmed her hiccups and left her only just weeping.

"Oh, I'm such a coward," Molly wept.

"No you're not," my mother said, "we won't let those jerks talk like that to us, honey darling, we'll not let them mean one thing because they don't and we'll just come right into that meeting together in the front with the two of us together and lookee you heah, me and you will see if they aren't just all talk and nothin' but a leel bit of shit on a stick, just you wait now, just you see, darling honey bunny darling girl, we'll show them we know they don't mean those horrible calls. . . ."

"But you, they'll, you can't just . . . ," Molly raised her head to say, for she knew anyone befriending a Communist in the fifties—when Hollywood went on TV in black masks, which was the last thing in the world I as a child would turn to on TV, but the only thing any adults wanted to watch all day—would make a suspicious citizen wonder if my mother was pink or my father was to be found as favoring Trotsky, and suppose those marked Americans informing on TV who were so stupid and talked like it was okay to interrupt when even I, by the age of ten, knew it wasn't, suppose one of those dreadful men in suits who looked so ugly and uninterestingly blank just beyond ugly were to notice who Trotsky was and not like it so my father would be an out-of-work musician blacklisted like Mitchell Craven and we'd be all in the Poor House together off somewhere at the edge of L.A. where all I'd do would be to eat tunafish sandwiches and brood that my mother's ability to pass unscathed through everything else till now suddenly turned out to have been merely the way a saint might seem who was not a saint but merely passing as one until suddenly she went too far which they never would have noticed if she'd stayed home from the PTA.

But no, she went to the PTA with Molly.

Naturally no one at the time (except Molly who had little sympathy with saints) even noticed that my mother might be doing a brave act because saints are lucky and don't have to be brave.

In school they tried to educate me to believe that life had nothing to do with luck but I was sorry for them and so was my mother.

When I went to Hollywood High it was run by a bunch of vicious virgins—sorority sisters—who maimed friends of mine for life, whether they made it or not, since once they tried to get in a club at all, they were finished. If you asked me, the only thing to do was to hide in the Girls' Room and smoke until the tenth grade was over with.

It was in the Girls' Room that first week I arrived at high school where I met Franny Blossom, smoking Kents.

"How can you smoke Kents?" I asked. "I mean, in here the smoke is so thick already it's like smoking Pall Malls anyway, how can you even taste Kents?"

She said, "Maybe I should smoke two."

Franny and I became friends that night when we smoked thousands of cigarettes and drank gallons of coffee and told each other everything in a coffee shop called Norm's on Sunset and Vine.

"I just moved to Hollywood," Franny said, "because before my father lost everything by being so drunk, we lived in Bel Air and you should have seen our peacocks. I went to a private school. Everybody was so rich. But now we're not."

"Golly," I said.

"My father drinks. Do you like Dexedrine? Here." She dropped about forty or fifty large Dexamyls into my purse so we never shut up for days.

"My mother was a cowgirl singing in a trio like a vaudeville act and my father was a holy roller missionary on his way to South America when he met my mother and fell from grace. He became a sinner when he and my mother got married. Because she made him leave the church and get rich. So now he drinks."

"Gee," I said, "it's just like Tennessee Williams, you're so lucky."

The day Franny took me to the house her parents owned when they moved out of Bel Air to Hollywood, I realized that I had never been up in that part of the Hollywood Hills before except once when I'd gone to a birthday party for the daughter of Roy Rogers and Dale Evans who sat next to me in school, and her house was a gigantic mansion.

But Franny's house had fourteen rooms and was just as gigantic to me, and it was all stucco and Spanish enamel tile and a cracked tennis court where Franny parked her old Cadillac ('52). (She was one of the few girls in school who even had a car.) The wishing well had a goldfish in it and the fountains even worked and there were four fireplaces, six bedrooms, and even a separate guest house with two stories and a bar.

There was a trellis with wisteria hanging from it, too.

I had met people like Franny's parents—people who drank Scotch with ice cubes—because kids I went to school with always seemed to have parents like that to spoil their childhood, but Franny's mother was different. And she didn't mind me either.

A lot of kids had parents who did mind me, so I could tell the difference.

When Franny and I began hanging around together in high school one of the best things about it was that we wore the same size and both were blond so we lived in and out of each other's purses practically as far as lipstick and mascara went since everything that looked okay on me did on her, too.

Of course I was more accessibly cute-looking to guys at first glance but once you saw her on stage when she lit up like the tail of a comet sprinkling across a galaxy in the night skies, people couldn't stand to look at anything else.

The first time I saw Franny act, rehearsing for a scene for her class, we were in her living room of that mansion she hated and I loved, doing the last scene from *Gigi* where she

tells the worldly suitor who wants to make her his mistress
that she'll do it only if he says he doesn't love her because
how could he love her if he sees the kind of life he'll be
letting her in for. Of course any actress who plays this part
has to A) convince you she's so adorable that she can make
mincemeat out of the Marquis de Sade, and B)convince you
that she's so perversely logical that she'd rather be with
someone who doesn't love her than a man who does as a
mistress. And C), she also has to convince you she's totally
right—and Franny did all of these things, *plus* at the same
time there was a sort of detached laughter of another, wiser
woman hanging over the entire idea of people who believed
actors on the stage.

"You know, Franny, you really are a star," I said, one night
driving home from Kelbo's.

"No, I'm not," she said. "If I were we'd move back to Bel
Air."

"And leave that house," I cried, "but I love that house."

"You do?" she said frowning as she thought about all that
revolting wisteria. "Well," she added, *"chacun à son goût*, I
suppose."

The truth was, I couldn't act at all, because anytime I had
to say someone else's words, they turned into marshmallows
sticking my mouth into lumpy resistance, refusing to blithely
tumble into the air like they should even in Beckett and not
just Shakespeare or Noel Coward, for whenever I had to
speak anyone else's words I put up a fight. *My* words, I deep
down thought, were just as brilliant and original as theirs
(*more* original in fact, since everybody had *heard* their
words, whereas they were just finding out mine that very
moment). I was just a lousy actress, in other words.

And yet whenever people saw the two of us together, people in those days always were determined to make me into a
star and they refused to even give Franny a screen test. They
had never seen her in scenes for her acting class the way I

had one day, doing a scene from *Saint Joan* and then singing "I'm Just a Girl Who Cain't Say No" for an encore.

Suddenly, when I met Franny, instead of having to survive the onslaught of those sorority sisters and try not to notice at Hollywood High, I became immersed in a kind of Sunset Strip–Beverly Hills world of actors, acting classes, little theater productions, metallic-green Cadillac convertibles, the clap, and drinks.

The first night Franny took me to Kelbo's, I'd never had a drink in a bar before because I was only fifteen and the law in California was that you couldn't drink unless you were twenty-one—and they meant it sincerely. Of course, Franny and I had gone down to Japan Town and bought sake in liquor stores because she figured that if white people couldn't tell how old Japanese people were, then they wouldn't know we were underage either, and she'd been right too—but drinking like an ultra-sophisticated woman with a cigarette holder and fake eyelashes sitting at a bar was beyond my wildest dreams before Franny took me to Kelbo's.

Kelbo's is still a tropical rum drink place in West L.A. on Pico and is famous for rum drinks but when Franny and I went there, the bartender was her own private Uncle George, who wasn't really her uncle at all but the man who'd been about to marry her mother when she ran off to San Pedro to marry the missionary, and Uncle George—who had been a "friend of the family" ever since—served us anything we wanted.

"But wasn't Uncle George jealous when your mother married your father?" I asked.

"By then, he was my father's best friend," Franny explained. "In fact, when my mother and father were married, Uncle George was my father's best man."

"God," I sighed green with envy, "just like Tennessee Williams all the time."

Uncle George had invented a special drink just for Franny called Heartbreak made out of champagne and framboise and grenadine which I thought was divine because it was cerise but Franny took one sip and frowned.

"This isn't a drink," she cried, "there's no alcohol in this!"

"What do you mean, champagne isn't a drink?" Uncle George said.

"Come on," Franny said, "what did you serve my mother last time? Something with rum in it? Something that's a drink!"

"Oh, okay," he said.

He returned with a tray on which a large ugly soup dish was supported by three barbaric-looking Tahitians made out of brown ceramic glaze. Inside the dish were floating ice cubes and lots of murky absinthe-looking liquid and on top were two gardenias like a lily pond.

"What's this?" Franny asked, her eyes widening with joy.

"It's called a Vicious Virgin," he said. "I just invented it."

Franny sipped it out of a straw which was nearly drowning in the lake.

She sighed, closing her eyes.

I took a sip too, it tasted like sharp lemonade.

"It's two kinds of brandy, five kinds of rum, and K rations of lemonade," he said.

By the time we'd gotten a quarter of the way through, we were feeling seasick. Before we could drive home, we both had to throw up for half an hour. The place was great.

"You'll never get into UCLA with those grades," Miss Karl of Hollywood High would say before I even sat down.

"Yes, I know," I replied.

"I'm Miss Karl," she now said, "sit down there. Facing me. I'm terribly worried about your future. And so should you be. That's what we're here to discuss."

Well, I was not about to discuss my decadent ideas about

how great it would be once I finally got out of school with a high school diploma with someone I'd never seen before in my life. Someone wearing a Kelly green scarf next to her face, making herself look dead.

"Uh-huh," I said.

"It's your attitude," she said, "you've no enthusiasm. No clearcut view of your life. No aims, no goals. You don't even have a major."

"Maybe Spanish?"

"You've got to have more of a plan in mind for where you want to be in five years, ten . . . ," she said.

"But I thought majoring in Spanish was okay," I said, confused.

"You haven't even taken shorthand, just typing," she said. "What good is typing, if you get a job in an office you're going to need more than that."

"My homeroom teacher told me I could get my major changed to Spanish even though I started with French and changed my mind," I pleaded.

She looked at me with disappointed eyebrows.

"How do you expect to get into college?" she said. "You can't major in Spanish, you've got to think about the future."

But it turned out that I could major in Spanish and graduate which was what I wanted to do and not all the tea in China or anything Miss Karl could say would make me spend my youth in any more school.

Of course, Franny Blossom disappointed them deeply too, because according to her previous school record, she was supposed to have an IQ of 190 and all she got once she arrived at Hollywood was C's or F's. They knew she wasn't living up to her potential.

Whenever I came home from one of these school counselor meetings, I'd ask my mother, "Mother, do I *have* to be anything?"

"Of course not, dear," she said.

"Well, what about money?" I asked.

"You can always live with us," she said.

Of course, my mother was always smiling benevolently at her company after dinner and saying, "I wish you could all come here and live with me for a year. That way I could make dinner for us like this every night."

Deep in her heart, the girl in blue wished the country could have another Great Depression so everybody would be thrown upon her mercy and she could rise to the occasion.

I once asked Lola about her attitudes and clearcut view of life.

"It was so awful," Lola would always say, "because I've never been able to persuade anybody of anything, you know —especially by logic. Intellectually I've always finished last. In the Hollywood School for Girls the teacher used to say, 'You are like a little butterfly fluttering outside but one day you must come in and face the truth.'"

"A butterfly?" I asked.

"And I couldn't help it because tears just ran down my face."

"Why, because of facing the truth?" I asked.

"No," Lola cried indignantly, "because I knew I'd *never* do it. I'd always be a butterfly. Or some kind of animal. God, that reminds me. . . ." She stood there a moment. We were about to sit down on the green grass under the windy hot blue L.A. sky in a little gully where no bagpipe drone could find us. "Once Agnes de Mille was doing a scientific study on hair follicles and how certain types of hair only grew on intelligent people. And she sampled my sister's hair but not mine. She just didn't even think I was there . . . That's what I was like there though, a complete butterfly fluttering outside in the flowers. . . ."

"Agnes de Mille was there?"

"And she was just as clumsy then too, poor thing," Lola said. "The girl was never able to move, you know, the simplest gesture eluded her. It was sad."

By the time Franny and I began drinking Vicious Virgins at Kelbo's, the vicious virgins running Hollywood High were very tame and though they tried to invite both of us to sorority teas or to sit at their bench during lunch, Franny and I were getting into so much trouble running around in black cocktail dresses with fake eyelashes and high heels night after night that school seemed hopelessly small time. To us both, the future was Hollywood.

At least when we got to Paris, we knew once and for all we'd get something to eat and after two weeks in London, I was finally beginning to look svelte as hell from starvation, so for the first time in my life I looked fashionable.

My father's musicological efforts had paid off and he'd gotten a Bach grant just in the nick of time (the Musicians' Union had just voted itself out of a job as usual and gotten rid of "that crook" who ran it so that suddenly it had *no* crooks on its side and it went straight to the dogs). In fact, my father had gotten *two* Bach grants—a Ford Foundation and a Fulbright—and suddenly, just as I was about to follow Franny into the movie business, my parents were dragging me off to have Interesting Experiences someplace almost as bad as New Jersey—Paris.

But on the train from Cherbourg, there was only scenery —no food—and my father kept promising, "When we get to Paris, we'll ask Sam for the best place to eat."

"*Sam!*" my mother said. "He's the one who can't even find a decent Chinese restaurant in San Francisco."

"Yeah, Daddy," I reminded him, "he smokes so much grass *everything* tastes delicious to him."

My father flinched, remembering what Sam's idea of great

Chinese food was in the restaurant he recommended we go
to in San Francisco one time when I was younger. And it
was not the kind of food a person like my father could gloss
over. I mean, food *is* food after all and it does have to get
stuck in to your mouth. So there was no getting around the
fact that Sam's place was all cornstarchy and lackluster and
piled high with rubber octopi for authenticity. But once you
got it into your mouth, Sam's definition of a good time bit the
dust.

The sky over Paris the night we arrived was glowing miles
above the city, like it actually was what my father said, "The
City of Light." Getting out of the train at the Gare du Nord
or wherever we were, I noticed something horrible about
Paris I never overcame, which was how short everybody was
except me—and my sister, who was already cuter than me
anyway, was now *in*.

In high heels I towered over everyone whereas Bonnie,
who was only five feet two to begin with, was already skinny
enough even before London to pass through the Left Bank
without them muttering to her what they did to me: "Alle-
magne."

"That means German," my father informed me, the second
time it happened the first five minutes we were in the train
station in Paris. "I guess they think you're so tall and blond
you must be German."

"Well, ick," I said. (I was only eighteen.)

My father got a *jeton* finally and tried to call Sam, but Sam
wasn't there. My father called another number, the number
of Steve Hoffner, a friend of Sam's, but Steve wasn't there
either.

"Well," I said, "I guess we better find our *own* food."

"We'll leave our things at the *pension*," my father said.

Luckily, we did not have to camp out like we did in Lake
Arrowhead when we were in Paris. It was nicer, like San
Francisco, we got to go places where there were beds and

chairs, and where we got to eat in restaurants, although this didn't do me any good since I was too tall to have any fun.

We were allowed to have our own private shared room, my sister and I, even if it was six flights up and overlooking the Panthéon. Naturally, the first thing we did was go number two in the bidet.

"Hey," my sister said, "this toilet doesn't flush."

I watched her try all the nozzles, but nothing budged the thing one inch. Finally we decided to wrap it in paper and put it on the balcony.

"Those toilets sure are funny," I casually mentioned to my father on our way to the restaurant at last.

"What toilets?" he asked.

"Oh, they mean the bidet," my mother said, looking at us and beginning to laugh. "What did you do with it?"

"We put it on the balcony," my sister said.

"The toilet is down the hall," my father explained.

"Oh," we both said.

"Here we are," my father said, "a fixed-price restaurant."

(That night when we came back from the restaurant, it wasn't on the balcony anymore where we'd left it wrapped up in the pages of *Paris Match* and we were certain it couldn't have fallen off the ledge from a six-story window or it would have landed on somebody's head—and we were sure things like that don't happen.)

In Paris, where all the women went to such extravagant lengths to look so chic, my mother won hands down. There was just something about the way she dressed that was always a little too outrageous—like her after-dinner cigar—to be merely chic, she was more than just that. She managed to put together a style eventually that was such a blend of Italian, French and L.A. fabrics and fashions that nobody on earth figured out how she got so avant-garde two years ahead.

Even that first night in the restaurant, before my mother had really had a chance to figure out the territory, she managed to outdo the fall season on the Left Bank women merely by the way she walked with such authority in her coat, which was pink on one side, yellow on the other, and blue in the back, which she'd created for herself out of baby-blanket remnants and lined with a flowered French silk print that somehow managed to look like a mixture of Dior and Joseph's "coat of many colors" from the Old Testament. It was the only place you could look in a room when she came in and the eye found it restful in spite of its audacity.

She also wore a fresh rose in her hair, shoved into her waist-length chignon and somehow staying put. While everyone in the restaurant stared at my mother, I finally and at last got something to eat without any further complications.

Then all I wanted was to climb the six flights and go straight to sleep until noon.

However, the first thing the next morning there was a knock on our door and I got up asking "Who is it?" instead of "Qui est là?" but that was okay because it was Steve Hoffner who spoke L.A. English.

"I'm sorry, I'm looking for Mort Lubin," he said.

"He's my father," I said, "are you—?"

"Look," he said, "I'm Steve Hoffner. Sam's friend. I'm sorry if I look like I've been up all night. But I've been up all night, with the police. They found Sam. In his apartment on the Boulevard Raspail. He was dead. Under suspicious circumstances. And they've quarantined the premises. Because of drugs. But I shouldn't be telling you, you're just a child, where's your father?"

"What's that?" I asked.

Steve Hoffner was lugging two of those insanely heavy containers you put film cans into so you can carry them around, weighing about twenty-four pounds each. Naturally he'd be a mess having carried two of those up six flights of stairs.

"That's what he wanted me to bring him, it's a print of his

latest—his last—film." Steve Hoffner looked like a meek accomplice, unequal to Sam's ordinary day-to-day escapades, never mind what he'd just pulled off this time.

"My father's up one more flight," I said.

"Oh," he said.

"I'll go get him," I said.

"Could you?"

I ran upstairs and knocked on my parents' door.

My mother opened it, looking annoyed and saying "Shhhhh, you'll wake your father."

"That Steve Hoffner's downstairs," I said.

"Who?" My father woke up.

"Something's happened to Sam" (although to me, it seemed this was simply another of Sam's usual tricks).

"To *Sam?*" my father asked, looking afraid.

"He's dead," I said.

"He's *what?*" my father asked, suddenly swept to his feet and in tears.

I couldn't really believe he was crying over Sam himself. I thought it must just be because somebody—anybody— he'd known was dead at all. The adults I knew seemed to cry when anybody died.

But how could they cry over Sam, I wondered silently, when they knew he was going to die anyway? I mean, for one thing anyone who takes heroin "for migraines" is bound to o.d. by accident sooner or later, especially in Paris where the heroin is so much better than Americans were expecting —*plus* if you asked me, o.d.ing in Paris was practically all there was to do.

Anyway, my first few days in Paris there was really too much to see to think about Sam. I only remembered that in the eighth grade I'd written an essay called "The Most Interesting Place I've Ever Been" which was about Sam's apartment in San Francisco after he left Lola. Aunt Helen had been staying there and Sam was out, but I remember being fascinated that anyone could live in a place where all the windows were papered over so no sunlight could possibly get in, the bookshelves were laced with Snickers Bars and English toffee containers, the bathroom was even ready in case there was a blackout. The floor was covered with Persian rugs, the couch was so low it was practically like the *Arabian Nights,* there was a hookah on the orange crate bookend, the lamps were definitely not encouraged to go above twenty-five-watt lightbulbs, and when I looked at it later, it was practically a classic dope-fiend's retreat. I got an A and I read the essay aloud in class.

"What an interesting place," my English teacher remarked.

"I thought so," I said.

Paris, though, looked to me like a graveyard after Sam died and ever since it seemed to fit and just be a continuation of that little cemetery where Sam was buried, crammed together in markers of gray; no matter how artistic or full of fol-de-rol the rest of Paris was, they still seemed only decorations on tombstones in their heart. For in the daytime the city was as gray as a cemetery and not made of light at all.

My poor mother thought that I would resign myself to having a great experience and stay in Paris after my parents left Bonnie and me there and went to Germany. However, luckily I didn't have to, since resigning myself had never been my idea of fun. And I had only been there two months (we were supposed to be there a whole year), when one day I was sitting in La Coupole reading my third Nancy Mitford about how great Paris was for snappy repartee (which, unfortunately, was lost on me), letting my mind wander back to the nostalgic mornings when Franny and I used to smoke Kents and eat hashed browns in a place near school called Snow White's, decorated by all seven Hollywood dwarfs,

97

making La Coupole seem lonelier than ever, until I looked up and suddenly Paris wasn't so bad—for there he was—Ed Lakey. *The* Ed Lakey. And this time I wasn't too square.

Whereas a year before at Hollywood High when I'd seen him on Alumni Day (he'd graduated ten years before), I had only been a miserable seventeen-year-old virgin unable to do anything but bump into him by mistake until finally he realized by the fourth time that it wasn't coincidence and looked at me with those silvery eyes as he said, "How about meeting me later at Snow White's?"

"Me?" I said, only I was too scared to come out of the bathroom till dusk, and now here he was and this time, thank God, I was depraved.

Ed Lakey at twenty-eight looked just like the dreamboat he had been when he went to Hollywood High—he was six feet two with this straight brown hair and this skin which looked like it would never tan because it was too bloodless —or more like his blood didn't have any red in it—and when he did get tan, it was sort of a pewter shade—as though he were really silver all the way through—but this only made him look scary or scarier, and a thing like that went a long way in Hollywood. Especially if you looked like the boy next door otherwise.

He was holding a *Herald Express* in his hands rolled up like a baseball bat when he saw me and as he recognized me and said, "I waited but you stood me up!"

"Let's have vodka gimlets," I suggested.

"It's ten A.M." He winced.

"What are you looking at me like that for?"

"Have you done any movies?" he asked.

"Don't tell me you're a producer," I said, "I'm *from* Hollywood, remember? Besides, I like you already."

"But I am a producer," he said.

"Couldn't we have vodka gimlets?"

"Why don't you meet me tomorrow," he said, "for dinner."

"Why not lunch? Now?"

"Because," he said, "I'm leaving for Rome in an hour."

"Rome?" I asked. "But what about *us*?"

"We'll have dinner here," he said.

He wrote on a card and handed it to me with the words Re Degli Amici scrawled on it as the restaurant in Rome and an official title of Executive Producer for some movie company in Cine Città—and he expected me to drop everything I was doing and go.

"What do I tell my mother?" I asked.

"Tell her I'm going to make you a star," he explained, waving his newspaper at any objections.

"Are you?"

"Why do you think I wanted you to meet me at Snow White's?" he asked, puzzled.

"For pleasure," I replied, "so I didn't come."

"Don't you want to be in the movies?" He frowned like it was frivolous to let love enter your mind when you could work all day instead.

"Do you give head?"

"Do I what?"

"Because otherwise what fun is it?"

(Nobody could ever accuse me of letting my career ambitions interfere with true values.)

"You're obviously not serious," he sighed, rising to his feet and walking to the Boulevard Raspail ready to make someone else a star. But then he came back and said, "You're the one ingenue who looks French enough I've seen in two weeks here."

"Me? They think I'm German," I said.

He lifted me to my feet in one motion, kissing me until Old Spice from his after shave came out of my toes like rainbows and I knew head was the least of my problems. It was all I could do to keep my pants on in broad daylight as it was.

"I've always wanted a vodka gimlet," I said. "Couldn't we just have one before we're too old?"

"Maybe some coffee," he said, looking at his watch.

"What's Cine Città like?"

"You're not going to stand me up again, are you?" he asked.

"Now?" I asked.

Since *La Dolce Vita* had come out in 1959 and it was 1961, it was not that great a time for eighteen-year-old girls to ask their mother if they could go to Rome, but after I sobbed for five days on the phone to Germany, my mother said, "Molly is there in case you get into any serious trouble."

(So naturally I never got caught.)

By the end of twenty-two hours on the train from Parigi to Roma, I was wondering if Ed was worth an entire continent without one burrito, but when I saw him I forgot everything but vodka gimlets.

We drove through Rome in this Alfa (red) from some year or other—a convertible—and the flying statues filled the sky every time we turned a corner except in Perioli where Ed lived which was too American for flying statues.

And except for Cine Città which did not look like San Juan Capistrano (as I had pictured it beforehand) but more like we were lost—which I was sure we were the first time I saw it and Ed stopped, because it looked like a deserted army barracks. Only Ed hadn't been asking directions, he was actually going in.

But it was fun that first day, getting ready for a screen test —dressed up like the Winged Victory (only with a head) and all made up to be a French ingenue—and I was perfectly sure I could float right into the movies—however for the next five hours all I did was sit getting dusty while Ed said I was being "lit."

"But why don't they just *make* the cameras go and to hell with the light," I exclaimed.

"Because," he said, "this has to be right."

Well, if you asked me, if a person didn't look cute enough to be a movie star without electricians getting their two cents in, the game wasn't worth the candle—only after about a week, when I realized that for every scene these same men took two days to figure out the lights—and it wasn't just me —I began to wonder just what difference lights made that kept rearing its endless interruptions so you couldn't just shoot—you had to come back tomorrow and hope they'd gotten it straightened out. It fascinated me that a person as obsessed as Ed Lakey could wait while the sands of time ran by for some Austrian light fixture coming over the Alps by truck.

In fact, how two such conflicting obsessions as ours could exist in the same line of work I never knew: Ed's, totally committed to a Movie Monk existence, finding out nothing unless it pertained to movies, reading newspapers only for situations which "might make a movie," looking at girls with that peculiar frame of values and judging them on whether or not they'd stay up all week to finish a movie and were On the Team, or whether they'd insist there was more to life than being rich, famous and immortal; and mine, which was to join the Navy and see the world. I mean, all I really wanted to know was whether I *could* be a movie star—not *be* one.

In the meantime, I lived in Rome where the statues flew in the air like clouds in this *pensione* called the Pensione Angelo where girls like me—starlets—and guys from Boston with guitars stayed and smoked Rothmans all day and walked over to the Rosati Bar every night to drink Campari and soda and where men told me about the reasons they had to leave New York and how they "bought" the Italian telephone operators for fifty dollars a month so they could make thousands of dollars' worth of calls a month. After all, Rome had been depraved for two thousand years and it wasn't about to slow down just because of the movie business—although if it hadn't had the flying statues, it might have made me homesick for Schwab's.

Ed did make me a star—or at least a star*let*—since although I actually was in movies, I didn't make the kind they paid stars to be in, unless they were over or under the hill (under was what I was).

Ed and I lived together the first week I was there and I was cured of ever wanting to live with him again and I had a pretty good idea that I was right when I was little to think that except for my parents, no two adults of the opposite sex should ever do anything but go for rides in the limo to the country with caviar and champagne, maybe for as long as a weekend perhaps ("There's a Small Hotel" made a big impression on me), but any longer than three days and it was sure to be curtains. The idea that "children needed a father" seemed to be what drove people to doing more than a weekend but, in the first place, who needed children if they were going to cramp your style by needing a father?

Of course, there were times I went to visit friends in the hospital in Rome who had hepatitis or broke their leg (which was practically the only way anybody learned Italian, since unless you got into an accident or were real sick, you hardly ever got into a situation where speaking Italian was a matter of life and death) and suddenly the most footloose vagabonds were totally changed into pillars of the community. Having been taken care of by some girl nobody ever imagined them with overnight, they'd move in with her, get married, and start saying things like "Giuseppa, our maid, is such a jewel."

But if you ask me, getting hepatitis was just about the only way I'd have been scared enough to learn Italian much less ever live back with Ed no matter how rotten my *pensione* was when it rained. And no matter how he pleaded it was what people in love should do.

The only time I looked at a newspaper in Rome was that summer Marilyn Monroe died all by herself in Hollywood when suddenly she became an indelible missing person on the cover of every newspaper and magazine in the world. It was half my lifetime ago since I'd seen her when I was ten cutting through the smog, but I'd been waiting for her to show up somehow again all that time and suddenly, she just stopped in her frame and her images went on without her. My mother later read a piece somewhere about how Monroe lived in a bungalow on the grounds of the old man, Joe Schenck, who was head of Fox—who'd had sheep's or goat's testicle shots in order to have sex and whom she kept waiting for as long as she could while she stayed in bed with some other guy so the shot would wear off. My mother told me that when she was married to Pietro her friend Billie took her to meet Schenck in this penthouse overlooking the Strip and that he asked Billie to encourage my mother to come back. And later, when getting into the studio orchestra at Fox was impossible because the head contractor was a Stalinist, an old man my mother knew who was a Spanish teacher told her, "You know Schenck? And you don't make him give Mort a job—*go* right over there," which my mother did. "The first few times I went just to show him my drawings but he wasn't interested in them, only me, so finally I asked him if he would please give my husband a contract. And three days later he called me up and said he had. And the next time I went to see him, they kept me waiting for twenty minutes in the office—which I read was how long Marilyn said it took for those shots to work—and when I came in, I knew something embarrassing was going on so I told him I was late for an appointment and left, but your father's contract was never rescinded—and he worked there for twenty years." ("What are tits for," I said to myself, "if not to look promising during business negotiations?") But the headlines in Italy only said MARILYN È MORTA.

103

"I could have saved her," Ed said bleakly.

"Oh, everybody thinks that," I said.

"But *I* could have," he insisted—and I had a feeling he was right. All Ed ever liked to do was flirt and work and he could do them both at once, so maybe he could have saved her.

"Well, I wish you had," I said.

"I wasn't there," he said.

"Nobody was," I said.

We drove to Milan that day and Ed kept sighing, "But she was on the team."

(To Ed, the world came in two parts: either you were on the team or not, and if you were on Ed's team, it meant that you had his undying loyalty so that he would always get you parts in films he cast. "Even," an amazed actor once remarked, "when he doesn't *have* to remember you, he still does.")

(One night before the Academy Awards Ed told me that if he got it he was going to say, "Well, the team did great this year and if we work real hard, barring accidents, we'll take it again next year." But he chickened out when he got the actual Oscar and just made the "I want to thank everybody" speech they all did.)

However, as much as loyalty seemed sexy to me and as much as Ed Lakey *was* sexy not just to me but to girls before he told them he was a producer when they simply assumed he was trying to pick them up, by the end of the second year I still couldn't bring myself to stay longer than overnight at Ed's or move in.

"But it's my birthday," Ed told me, "and besides, your floor is under water."

"Just when it rains," I said (although it rained six months a year).

Every so often I would have to go over to the Cravens' and deliver a Christmas present or something for my mother.

After Mitchell was blacklisted and couldn't get work in Hollywood he was teaching in the American School in Rome which wasn't what he did best since he was really a wonderful actor—but the rest of the time I simply blocked them out and avoided that part of Old Rome where I thought I might run into Molly. Shelly was at Berkeley (where I once saw her the time we went to visit Estelle) but if the Cravens had had their way, she would have gone to Smith or Radcliffe and been educated enough for motherhood like everybody from Connecticut was in those days. But usually I forgot to ask my mother how she was since I blocked Shelly out too.

It was the Christmas when Ed had gotten me on the covers of *Epoca* and *Oggi* (for this horrible big-deal B movie promotion we were doing), plus any other stray movie magazine in either four-color or black and white that he could talk into it.

It was freezing rain outside when I arrived at Molly's in person (which my mother insisted upon, otherwise she turned into a snake), and I rang the bell as I shivered under my umbrella.

"Well hello, Sophie Lubin," Molly said, opening the door to her palazzo apartment (a cheap palazzo).

"Merry Christmas," I said as best I could. (The funny thing was, I was glad to see her.)

"Oh, are you coming in?"

"Well, I . . ." I came in, otherwise you had to shout.

"I'd offer you a cookie, but I don't want you to get warm or you'll just catch cold because you have to leave right away."

"Here's your presents," I said.

"Put them there, they're wet, don't set them down where they'll stain," she said.

"How's—"

At which point Mitchell himself cheerfully appeared, and it was so great to see him I stopped frowning.

"You should be in school," Molly said. "What are you doing?"

(It would take Molly, of course, to live in a town with me on the front page of every glaring tabloid and refuse to look at it or notice that I was otherwise employed.)

By that Christmas I'd been in Rome two years and one nice (not raining) morning, perhaps in March, I was on my way to meet someone, walking to the other side of the Tiber. I had on my usual tweed skirt and too-tight sweater over my too-L.A. breasts and my usual five-inch heels that made me six feet tall, and I was heading toward Hadrian's Tomb, standing at an intersection where I was towering over almost everything but the Castel Sant'Angelo itself, when all of a sudden I felt this tugging at my side, like a gnat.

I looked around and there, down on the sidewalk looking up, was a tiny man, about a foot and a half shorter than me, who was dressed like a bum, and through his tiny little wire-framed glasses he was staring way up at me.

It gave me the most awful feeling, being that blond and healthy and rich and Southern California-perfect in this tiny man's eyes anyway, and I took yard-long lunges across the intersection when the light turned green and was almost out of breath two blocks later when I finally allowed myself to slow down, knowing I'd been far too fast for him to catch up.

But just as I was coming to the bridge, the tiny man appeared in front of me, having somehow managed to know some shortcut or to rematerialize at will, either one.

Seeing him there, just a few paces in front of me, really made it even worse and I actually began to run as fast as I could, which was pretty fast, even if I was wearing such high heels. But the moment I allowed myself to relax after crossing the bridge and gotten two blocks away, there he was—in front of me again.

Only this time I stood there and did not run.

This time I calmly reviewed all the Italian I possibly could drum up.

Instantly, the phrase appeared perfectly in my mind and I conjugated it especially for him so he'd know who I meant.

"*Basta* and *ciao ciao bambino*," I said imperiously.

It was as though I'd hit him with a club, like I was Aphrodite and he a mere mortal, and here the goddess of Beauty and Blondness had slammed him one for no reason at all. He flinched and tears squeezed out of his eyes and ran down his cheeks underneath his glasses as he drew back against the wall, mute.

Then he ran away.

And I decided to leave Rome right away.

I hadn't felt that bad since I gave Tango away.

Ed got me a fishy ticket (leaving from Frankfurt so I could say goodbye to my parents and landing in New York so I could say hello to Aunt Helen).

"Is this a black market ticket?" I asked.

"Shhh," he said. "And it's round trip, I need you back."

"Oh," I said.

As we were leaving my *pensione* he looked back and said, "Oh, there are your new boots. Now I know you'll come back. Soon."

(I couldn't exactly bring myself to tell Ed Rome didn't seem right anymore.)

In the taxi he looked up from the *Daily American* (he was now thirty, really *old*) and said, "It won't be any fun without you here."

"You know, Ed, why isn't Mitchell Craven on the team?"

"Who?"

"You know, he got blacklisted," I said, "he's really distinguished. He'd be great for the guy's uncle, the rich one?"

"Wait a minute," Ed said, slowly writing it down, "where can I reach him?"

I gave him their phone number.

Even though I knew I would never come back to Rome again, giving Ed Mitchell's phone number atoned for the feeling I got when I told that old man to *ciao ciao bambino*, and it made me feel just like me again whereas before I felt afraid I was turning into Sam, turning on someone who just loved me. Or whatever it was he did.

T HE TOWN OF HOBOKEN, New Jersey, where Aunt Helen lived, was not atoned for by Frank Sinatra. Fortunately, I already knew what to expect from Hoboken because we passed through it on our way to London, and the first day I'd seen what Hoboken looked like with my own eyes before I'd broken and run for it, getting to the Village in New York City all by myself on a bus before I called my parents and explained where I'd be after I picked up a guy from Yale (an actor) and had a place to stay.

So it didn't surprise me to see Aunt Helen standing in that drab little kitchen overlooking a grimy backyard which faced somebody else's grimy backyard behind someone else's little kitchen. And it didn't surprise me that her four children spoke with foreign New Jersey accents and not like they were from L.A. or her children at all.

"Ten years you've tried to live here," I would say to her after we lit a joint and had half of one giant Hershey bar with almonds, "and look at it—it's still fucking New Jersey!"

"Yeah, but . . . ,"she said dreamily.

It was obviously meant to be forgotten—New Jersey—as anyone could see just by looking at her.

"Darling dear," Helen said, changing the subject, "these boxes are so heavy."

"I'll say," I said, "those sixteen-millimeter cans weigh a ton and so does the film."

"What are you carrying such things for?" she asked.

"They're Sam's," I said, "I'm taking them to L.A. We can't figure out what to do with them."

"Doesn't he want them?" she asked, her voice so flushed with interest that all at once I knew she didn't know he was dead.

"Don't you know?" I asked her.

She looked at me with her large brown eyes, my sister's eyes and my father's eyes all the way from Russia, and panic branded through her usual haze forcing her to slump against the kitchen sink.

"No, I don't know," she said, "is he . . . ?"

"Of course," I said, "he's been dead for two years. Didn't anybody write you? Heroin or something."

She grabbed a dish towel and wept, flinging herself down into a chair so her elbows could rest on her knees.

"God, that's right! You had a crush on him too," I said, filled with wonderment once again at how peculiar adults always were. I mean, Sam was much too short for her anyway. How could anybody let themselves get a crush on a shrimp like Sam?

It was too dismal to stay in New Jersey any longer once Aunt Helen found out about Sam so instead I took a cab back to the airport and got on the first plane for L.A. We landed just at 6:oo P.M., the huge orange sun hung over the Pacific Ocean reflecting the sunset to anyone in the sky looking down as I was, and I was suddenly uncertain about what I would do. I thought perhaps I ought to call Goldie or some relative, but then I didn't want to be at the mercy of relatives so I took the bus into Hollywood and got off at the Hollywood Roosevelt Hotel where I couldn't get a room.

Suddenly I found myself alone in Southern California with no friends and hardly any money, lost and planless with no place to spend the night. The Cravens were in Rome of course, Franny was living on Martel in a West Hollywood bungalow court with three girls on the make for Marlon Brando—which gave me a headache whenever I thought

about it—Ophelia was up in Berkeley getting "an educa-
tion" although once you knew how to give head the way she
taught me I thought you didn't need to learn anything else
to get through life. Every time I thought about Aunt Helen
crying that way, I wondered if Lola had heard or if Sam was
going to surprise her like that too.

Once I got enough quarters from the lobby newsstand, I
telephoned Lola in San Francisco before going another step
on my planless way.

"I thought you were in Rome!" Lola said. "Where are
you?"

"I came back to L.A.," I said, "Hollywood."

"Oh, you kid," she said, "your poor mother."

"Listen," I said to her, screwing up my tact in case I was
supposed to handle myself like an adult, "have they told you
about Sam?"

"Oh, sure," she replied, "Steve Hoffner wired me from
Paris. I wasn't in the least surprised. Not in the least."

"Whew," I said.

"Oh," she said, "that's right. I can put two and two together, you know. After all, you were there."

"We got there but we didn't see him," I said. "He sort of
was dead before he knew we were there."

"What a shame," Lola said, "I'm sure he would have liked
to see Mort. He would have put it off for one day if he'd
known."

It occurred to me that she believed Sam had purposely
o.d.'d rather than accidentally be taken by surprise, at least
she sounded like she thought he'd done it himself and could
just as well have waited as not.

"When did you get in?" Lola asked.

"Just now," I told her. "I don't know where I'm going to
spend tonight, I could stay at Goldie's, but that husband of
hers this time is such a—"

"I know," Lola agreed, "why don't you call Estelle? She's

staying in Marie's apartment while they're in Africa. And you know Marie lives around the corner from Barney's Beanery."

"Oh, goody," I said. "Goody, goody gumdrops."

"What was wrong with Paris? And Rome?"

"They're just never L.A.," I explained.

"Oh."

Lola then gave me Estelle's number and we said goodbye.

"*Ciao*," I said.

"*Ciao?*" she said. "Oh, your poor mother. *Hasta luego.*"

Somehow Helen's awful husband kept her stranded. New Jersey was as far from real life as the Evergreen Cemetery in Boyle Heights to me. Once I'd spoken to Lola and fallen straight back into the Hollywood I knew you could always go home to again, I felt everything come right back into focus. L.A. was not much at night but during the day it had become the city of light, the center of world culture and the arts and the smart money knew it. Even cars flourished in this sunny clime. If you were looking for a place to die, you'd go to Paris.

T HE PEOPLE WHO RENTED OUR HOUSE in Hollywood when we went to Europe did not pay rent for eleven months. The father and mother and daughter had a drawerful of bills in the kitchen in the middle drawer where my father used to keep hammers and tacks, bills for the telephone as it lapsed longer and longer, bills from us, letters from my father's accountant, bills from Michigan where they lived before coming to L.A., bills from Wisconsin where they lived before Michigan, bills from dentists, bills duplicating bills with NOTICE or IMPORTANT or LAST NOTICE DUE written in red across them—tons of bills.

Naturally, they looked excruciatingly respectable—not like us at all. We looked like disreputable bohemians to everyone with an ounce of *Reader's Digest* in their blood, but my father did not believe in credit, he believed in paying bills once a month before the crooks who owned the phone company began getting uppity.

Right after I returned from Rome, when everyone else in my family—my father, mother, and sister—were still in Europe, my father finally had been able to get rid of them but not until after they'd called the electrical wiring people working for the city and had our house condemned.

Of course, my father was a little weird about electrical wiring, I'll admit. I mean, no house in the whole world is going to have lights where he thought they ought to be— behind the pillow on his side of the bed, in the middle overlooking his other shoulder (to prevent eyestrain), on my mother's side of the bed, on both sides of the mirror on the downstairs stairwell, lights to be directly blazing over everything and lights to be indirect so people could talk to each other—the lights which blazed were for people whom he wanted to show something to in the living room, and the indirect lights were for after he'd shown them and they needed to rest up.

But once they got our house condemned, they lived on for another seven months before finally—a week before I returned to L.A.—they took all the lightbulbs and left.

In Heidelberg where my parents were staying unable to do anything but sit there while the tenant in our house complained about the fire hazard in outraged indignation, my father would say, "When the guy told me he was a Quaker I knew something about him was too good to be true. He's a crook—the same story that crook from Whittier uses, like Nixon. The same story both guys. Both crooks!"

"But darling . . . ," my mother would say.

"I'm selling the house," my father decided, "that's it!"

Of course, now that our house had been legally declared unsafe, even after the tenants left we could no longer let anyone new rent it unless the whole house was rewired and the city inspector declared it safe again, and since my parents were not able to oversee the job themselves, there was little else my father could do but sell.

But basically he was so mad at the house for being outraged in such a manner that he had to avenge himself by getting rid of it. Out of spite.

If our house offended him, fuck the goddamn thing.

Of course the whole episode ravaged our family—it was like having a foot amputated—at least it ravaged me in some mortal irrevocable way.

The past was torn off right there.

And from then on I would never feel exactly at home anyplace I lived. But then I never was exactly at home so to have felt so would have been wishful thinking.

Nobody in my family ever came home in time to see our house before it was sold but me. The place which I returned to was no longer home, of course, it was newspapers piled up in the corners and dust like gray clouds left to grow everywhere. There were curlers in the music room and bobby pins on the fireplace mantel on top of more stacks of bills. And there were brushes stuck in cans of paint in the dining room where someone had chosen school green to cover the roses on the wallpaper of half a wall, their one attempt to improve our house.

The only people who would buy our house, if they came in and saw it the way it looked that day, would have to be people who could envision the whole thing perfectly and have no sense of smell. For in spite of the refrigerator door closed sealing the smell of rotting chili off in a scentproof vacuum, the four days the chili had been left inside without the icebox turned on had managed to smell the whole house up anyway.

If I opened the refrigerator door even a crack, the smell no longer mattered, I decided, because it became scentless once it turned into simple pain.

Once a smell is just pain burning your respiratory tract, the scent no longer bothers you.

The only people who'd be capable of buying our house would be someone who just wanted the land and would tear the place down so they didn't care. Because anybody looking at that mess, seeing it the way the Quakers had abandoned the place, would be overcome by the willies.

And I couldn't let our house be flattened.

I owed it to our house to keep it a house.

And since occasionally, if no one is looking, I suddenly become good out of the blue, I did so that day. I alone was left holding the fort.

I cleaned that house up. I made it look nice. I closed my eyes and wrapped my nose in a washcloth and took the chili to the toilet where I flushed it to the sea so it could kill the sharks. I loaded all the newspapers into the trash and I used Ajax on everything from upstairs to downstairs and on the stairs themselves. When I left that night, the whole house looked relieved.

And when I returned in the morning to put finishing touches around on the woodwork and bathrooms, the smell was gone too. It was wonderful. The house was at home with itself once more.

It was the least I could think of to do, the debt I felt was in some way repaid.

The first people who saw the house bought it.

And that was the end of home.

Since then, I've had trouble looking at things that are too beautiful because they're only bound to wilt, or fade, or die —the longer you wait the more certain it will be.

So I try and always do two things at once, so as to get

around going too deep. Like wishing our house goodbye but at the same time washing the stairs.

WHEN I SAW FRANNY the day after I came home from Rome, I nearly choked on the waste of it all—her whole talent lying there untested in that little bungalow court she lived in on Martel. She was working part time in this little library around the corner in West Hollywood—like Garbo working as a dishwasher—and the dustiness over her eyes, living room, and dreams made me want to take her outside like a Persian rug and whack her with a broom.

But for two years she'd been baking senseless in the smog, getting rejected day after day, because she was too perfect-looking for the tiger-lady sixties and she was too sympathetic, cheerful, and Nathaniel Hawthorne for that place— she was impossible to cast.

"I don't know," Franny repeated over and over that first afternoon, pouring some more brandy into our glasses, her room as evening came lit by a candle, "maybe people like me are out for good."

"No!" I cried. "You're *great!* I know you're great. Look at you in *Gigi!*"

"Oh," she sighed, "I don't know."

But a day before I was supposed to go back to Rome after I'd redone the old house, I suddenly *did* know.

"*I* know," I said, "I know *exactly.*"

I explained how easy it would be to Franny and she looked at me and her eyes blinked three times, and she was filled with the champagne of adventure as she said, "But you're sacrificing your career."

It was easy really.

And besides, we were so young, we didn't know that just

because we were minors didn't mean they'd not lock anyone traveling on anyone else's passport up in jail like a normal felon—or an international violator of the Geneva code or something.

And besides, we went to Kelbo's on the way to the airport and by the time Franny got her hair messed up enough, she looked so much like me in my trenchcoat that she got right past the passport lady with my passport and into the plane without a backward glance, while I had her driver's license just in case anyone stopped me in her old Cadillac I'd always wanted.

The really amazing thing was that my *pensione* room in Rome and Franny's bungalow in Hollywood were both $87.50 a month.

And anyway, I didn't do it for her, I did it for a burrito which was all I wanted to eat finally.

I guess when Ed saw her in my boots, he figured she was on the team because he put her in the part he was going to give me, only with her, not only did she dub her own voice, she did two of the children and one old man.

THE FIRST MONTH or so I was back, I flew up to stay with Lola a week in San Francisco, because Luther was out of town and Lola and I wanted to hit all the thrift stores before they ran out of thirties satin nightgowns (which were twenty-five cents each). But first, we always had to go to the shop Frank Lloyd Wright designed in Maiden Lane where they sold crystal and the place was lit from the ceiling (made out of thick translucent glass) and it had an inside spiral going up to the second floor like the Guggenheim Museum. Among all this crystal and glass were always the Crazy White Cats who lived there—and whom I came to San Francisco because of (next to Lola).

"I've never seen cats who didn't knock everything down," Lola said, while one was purring in her arms and another was letting me pet it on a glass table. "Do you think that's why they're called crazy?"

"Why was Sam so mean?" I asked. "Speaking of crazy."

"He wasn't mean—at first—at first he was just crazy about *me*, you know, but you know, he liked cats better than people. He told me women had no souls."

"He *did!*" I cried. "Was he right do you think?"

"And he said dancers were the only ones stupider than musicians," she added, "but neither had any brains. Which was too bad."

"Why?"

"Because he never got to hear me play the violin," she said, "in fact, getting married would have been perfect for playing the violin."

"But I thought you had already given it up after the Mendelssohn fiasco more or less," I said.

"No, no, no," she said, "I still played it—and a lot better than some men I might add."

"You know," I said, "I still don't understand why anyone gave Sam the time of day."

"He had eyebrows like an Arab," Lola said.

"Tell me again about the time you were wearing the blue taffeta dress," I sighed, as Lola's cat slid to the floor and we both began strolling down to the first floor, and once again the tales of the Dinky, the street lamp, and the Mendelssohn *interruptus* soothed me in a way no other people's descriptions of the past ever could. If there was one thing about Lola's stories, it was not only that they had no moral, they were also completely devoid of ambition. (Even the girl in blue got out of Sour Lake.) Or at least any other ambition than to make as much of the moment as possible.

"Was he right do you think," I wondered, "that we don't have souls?"

"But we're from Los Angeles," Lola shrugged, "we had too much else to think about."

"But Sam was from Los Angeles," I said.

We both slowed down walking down the sidewalk, as Lola inhaled and let her breath release, saying "Men."

In 1963, when I was twenty, girls my age could either get married and live happily ever after or else fade into oblivion and become spinsters. Since living happily ever after was out for me once I spent the first week in Rome with Ed when I discovered he didn't wring out his washrag and fled one Sunday (only to be informed by the other girls I talked to that Ed was nothing compared to guys they knew who pee'd in the sink—in fact, Ed was a prince), I decided it was better to fade into oblivion right away and got a job as a cashier at the Oriental Theater not far from my bungalow—the perfect job for the rest of my life as a spinster, I decided.

Or at least until I recovered from not being Marilyn Monroe which had thrown me into such a brown study after two years in Rome that I needed a simple job.

I loved tickets: pink tickets, blue tickets, even yellow under-twelve-years-of-age tickets. I loved the way they smelled and how they looked in rolls—almost like reels of film—it seemed inspired, both rolled up into seeing a movie.

Besides, I was not bad. After all, I was a hot tomato all over Italy and it was the same thing at work at the Oriental only in English; it made me feel like I was under glass being in the ornate box office gazebo, a curly blond bed-doll like my mother found from the twenties with a beauty mark, cleavage, and little floppy bed-doll moues, lowered eyelashes and girlish blushes and I was like Dillinger, surrounded by men out to get me.

The Oriental was a "neighborhood" theater, only since the neighborhood was West Hollywood, the neighbors were Jack Nicholson and Stravinsky. I ran into nuns from Immaculate Heart in line too, and married couples, people on dates, lonely movie stars sneaking in to see themselves fourteen times a week, artists wrecked on mescaline who came for the cartoons, people of "the industry" and kids from Hollywood High just down Sunset a few blocks.

Before my bell jar gazebo passed the best minds of my generation, to say nothing of the cars. Lotuses and Rolls-Royces and chopped Plymouths and immense convertibles went back and forth, back and forth, before my eyes, with people inside—Afghans, ladies with blond hair spread a yard on either side of them, and men—elegant men, crisp sophisticated originals (including Cary Grant), James Dean slouchers, mad Marlons, confidential smoothies, awkward European guys who wore sandals with socks, slinky invisible guys whom girls committed suicide over.

If you asked me, for the first year or two it was enough. I mean, *plus* they paid me.

Anyway, I have always been one of those people who are grateful not to be in Siberia.

"Oh my what a lovely job you've got here," Lola said when seeing me in my proper setting—the usherette uniform at twilight when my light went on. "Oh your poor mother."

"Poor men you mean," I said. "No, tell me how you like it with my hair over one eye!"

"De-*lish!*" she exclaimed.

"Isn't it fabulous?"

"I never had anything half so much fun," Lola said, "even when I sold lingerie at the City of Paris."

Of course Lola was the one person I knew who could look at that job and realize the possibilities, and perhaps without Lola I might have struggled through life without a source of inspiration who was actually living, since in history the only jobs for women that sounded fun to me were the courtesans in Athens who just entertained brilliant men all day with their beauty and wit—or having a salon like Madame Récamier and entertaining all the brilliant men with her beauty and wit (only poor Madame Récamier, unfortunately, was stuck being married to a stodgy banker, besides, so after all I preferred being a plain courtesan because at least no bankers were there cramping your style). I read *Aphrodite* by Pierre Louÿs and the life of a courtesan sounded like just the thing.

I wanted to be perfect in every way—looks, wit, and expertise—however, once I was perfect, I didn't intend to let any man catch me. I wanted to be unattainable.

At least that's how I looked at it. I mean, unless you could have a job like I did where everybody in L.A. could actually *see* how perfect you were, a job was just going to clutter your mind with hysterical details like politics. I mean, how could someone expect you to vote when you were beautiful and had so many different outfits to wear? And so many boyfriends.

Anyway I had it covered both ways because I was perfect plus I was a spinster so all I had to worry about was my image.

Of course, the word *image* was already wrecked out of all proportion by pollsters and politics and *Time* magazine, but in the movie business—which God knows I was nearly indistinguishable from—image still conveys the whole set, not just "charisma."

I read one time that in the thirties a casting director in one of the main studios classified movie actors—both women and men—as what they projected on screen to an audience in the way of a lay and that Jean Harlow, for example, would be a "Good-Hearted Lay," while others were "Virgin Lays," "Exotic Lays," "Aristocratic Lays." And even "Tennis Lays." ("Tennis Lays" I couldn't figure.)

Friends in the early sixties must have thought I was another Marilyn Monroe Memorial Lay—which I was—especially after Rome when I yelled at the little man and made him cry. It made me really think for the first time in my life about horrible things like responsibility, which I never imagined would come up if all I was was a starlet, but which obviously was lurking even in bright curls, since provokingly bright curls are *bound* to provoke someone from the audience like that little man into thinking you are the Angel of Light and expecting you to be merciful. And if you aren't, then no wonder they thought Hollywood was phony.

So either I had to quit looking like that or else *become* that, and since it was easier to keep on bleaching my hair than to let it grow out and just keep on being merciless, I decided to follow the path of least resistance and do things like give away Mitchell's phone number to Ed.

(Only I made Ed promise never to tell Mitchell or he might really suspect what my mother was worried he thought about that day already, when the FBI arrived at my mother's front door asking for my father—asking about any Trotskyites around our house—but my mother Southern-belle'd it out, ". . . only when they left," she said, "they went straight across the street right to the Cravens' house, and that was the day Mitchell got blacklisted—but they must have had his address right there with them so they were going there anyway. My God, how could anyone think *I* told them anything?" If I did Mitchell too great a favor atoning for being merciless to that little man, it might look like I was trying to make up for something much worse.)

Anyway as my mother once said, "I don't know anything about politics—or rather I know too much to care." ("And *besides*," she added, "nothing works.")

However, I felt oafish enough doing a good deed, but having to explain you had no ulterior motive and were just doing a good deed out of contrariness was more trouble than even contrariness was worth.

In fact the only way a good deed didn't look oafish was

when it went by so fast it seemed like an accident and you didn't know who to thank anyway.... (Presents, on the other hand, should be wrapped so they wouldn't be mistaken for accidents.)

Perhaps the thing I liked best about being perfect of course was that in those days it made women an inspiration for men, so men could be geniuses. Since not only was it a family tradition to inspire men, but also the only way I could hang out with the artists in Barney's Beanery, I was supremely certain that what I was doing was not just fun, but noble.

Which was why I went out every night and made sure to go to a lot of parties, since it's no good being an inspiration if no one knows.

Anyway it helped to be responsible if I seemed hell-bent-for-leather since nobody suspected it was just a red herring and most people thought of me as a tornado.

A hot tomato tornado.

But meanwhile, underneath it all, all I wanted was the American Dream, to get my parents a bigger house than they got me.

About a week after I was twenty-one, Goldie took me to lunch at Musso's to celebrate my birthday late and while we were on our second drink she wanted to know what I was doing with my life, and since it seemed like a nice time for us to open a restaurant, a place where people in L.A. could sit down, I asked her if she was interested.

"But I have a job," she cried. "I hate cooking!"

"That's okay," I explained, "nobody's eating these days anyway, they're taking diet pills, we can open just a bar."

Goldie had looked awful ever since Mad Dog Tim left her in Watts and she moved into Hollywood with Ophelia and got a job in a Christmas card factory and married her third Trotskyite husband, the nice one. But she looked at least seventy years old or forty or some age like that which wasn't becoming, and her nice husband was such a stodgy influence that even when I was seventeen and didn't want to go to New Jersey, I wasn't willing to risk having him get mad at me for something like marijuana just because it was a silly felony.

Goldie, I decided, had had no fun at all for too long, and she ought to have, since being serious didn't become her coloring.

"We'll open our own restaurant," I told her abruptly.

"We what?" She actually laughed aloud, looking much younger in spite of wearing so much navy blue.

"That's right," I cried, "our own place, for everybody, *le tout d'L.A.!*"

"Well, do you think really ... ?" By this time, Goldie (whose black hair had already fallen down her back after her third martini, although it had been severely knotted when she came in) had lipstick marks on all three glasses growing fainter and fainter, but then I too was on my third martini (being twenty-one was so educational), and there we were, both drunk. Most of the people by then were gone as it was nearly three, which was the earliest I'd so far been so drunk so fast. The place was a large warm red-leather and varnished-wood cavern with those Belgian hunt murals not painted by the WPA (or they'd have been on the fox's side), and we both had delusions of grandeur or I never could have gotten her to quit her job—she just got up and telephoned saying she was not going back to the Christmas card factory tra-la ever again. (She'd only gotten the job anyway out of loyalty to Mad Dog Tim.)

By the next day though, Goldie changed her mind, calling me up to say, "I can't make sandwiches, much less start a restaurant, I'm very sorry, but I can't."

"Oh," I replied, "you? Sorry?"

"But you were so great, getting me to quit that job, all I've wanted to do for years is teach dance and now I'm doing it."

"You are?"

"I've put a deposit on Teretsky's old studio, it's just a mess now," she laughed, "but after we clear it out, you'll see, it'll be great."

"Is that where you first met Lola?" I asked.

"We all danced there," she said, "but you know, I haven't woken up looking forward this way since those days."

It was awfully close, because if Goldie hadn't had dancing to fall back on, I'd have wrecked her life if you asked me.

"At least somebody in the family has some common sense," she decided, "but nobody on my side. Maybe you inherited it from your mother."

"Me!" I cried, mortified.

"Or psychic, or something," she said.

"Oh," I replied, relieved since Goldie obviously didn't know what common sense was if she got it mixed up with psychic.

But Goldie was one of the easier ones since there were other well-meaning friends and relatives who weren't so easy to lose.

There was my father's friend Robert and his wife Lenore who collected real estate and only took me to fancy places like the Scandia. Robert said, "How can you waste your time on something that won't make money?"

"Didn't you used to write plays?" I asked.

"Never mind," Lenore said, "you've got to take some class —just something—instead of just drifting."

"Maybe I'll take . . . photography," I said, "like Sam."

"I hear you got there too late," Robert said.

"Did you know him?" I asked.

"We're not here to talk about Sam," Lenore said.

"You knew him, didn't you?" I asked her.

"When we lived in San Francisco," Lenore said, looking at her shoes, "briefly."

And there was my Aunt Lily who suggested the physical therapy class, my own friend who decided computer programming school was for me, and tons of other people who started telling me what to do and couldn't stop. Maybe I made people nervous by refusing to worry about anything, but I always knew everything would be okay because if worse came to worse I could always be a mistress. Or something with sin involved. And how anybody could look at me and think I'd be anything else when my hair was almost like Brigitte Bardot's I never knew. Sometimes they forgot we were in Hollywood.

But I was already much further into HOLLYWOOD than most of my parents' friends. It was like all they ever knew was the movies about Hollywood whereas to me the Sunset Strip was ten times more immediate than a movie. Plus it was alive.

And before rock'n'roll took it over, it was straight out of *Guys and Dolls* only with huge convertibles and rum drinks. And men with guns. And girls with black gloves up to their elbows in the daytime. (Even *I* wore them.)

So when they asked me if I considered working for the telephone company, I couldn't help it if I made them nervous, I refused to worry about jobs when Sunset Boulevard was a block away.

And of course there was always Grandma who accused me of not getting married because I was trying to kill her.

"Oh, shut up," I replied.

"Each day you're like a knife in my heart," Grandma added.

"Another one!" I asked.

"What do you mean?"

"Everything anyone ever did, you say that about," I said, "I'm surprised it worked on anyone even back then."

(But of course, Grandma was still poised and ready to wreck anyone's life in a big way, old-fashioned or not.)

"Tell me what Helen was like," I said.

"Oi, she was so miserable when she got married, it was a tragedy," Grandma began.

(But who made sure she got married? . . .)

Ophelia confessed to me, "I never knew what to do either, so I got married."

"I'm saving that as a last resort," I said.

"But you know so many men," Ophelia said, "isn't there even one for you?"

"They're all adjectives," I said, "they all make me feel modified; even a word like *girl friend* gives me this feeling I've been cut in half. I'd rather just be a car, not a blue car or a big one, than sit there the rest of my life being stuck with some adjective."

"Oh," said Ophelia.

"Friends I don't mind," I said. "But how can you stop at just one? There are so many."

But I knew that some people thrived on stopping at one like my parents. In fact, being together seemed to make each of them greater. Now if that was how anyone modified me, I could see it might not be so bad. But waiting was fun too.

The place I lived on Martel was sort of a mixture of Versailles and pagodas—I mean, it sort of looked like it was laid out in some kind of grand scale because the large house in the middle where originally a family who ran the place must have lived was built to make them feel like kings of all they surveyed, just like Marie Antoinette except that instead of it being as far as the eye could see which was the plan at Versailles, this place was surrounded by a court of bungalows which made it impossible to see out further than the immediate courtyard itself—because even if they tried to look out the front windows at the street, they were stopped by this trellis which was like Franny's old house, only this one ran twice as long in front and was overgrown not with delicate wisteria tangles, but with those little lavender bush flowers (which also grow in Florida where the town of Lantana became the home of the *National Enquirer*), but by then the trellis had caved in from so much lantana when it rained. The rooftops of the main house and bungalows were decorated with wooden pagoda ornaments painted chocolate brown to blend with the stucco walls which were sort of a chocolate-milk shade. And the wishing well in front had fish in it.

It was just the kind of place people who've never lived in Hollywood before have to get out of their system before they find an ordinary place with a garbage disposal and windows that close and let the dream be rented anew. But once I moved in myself, I never ever wanted to move again (except to the Normandy Towers which was a castle out of *Sleeping Beauty* and crazier than Disneyland, only whenever a place was vacant, I was always too broke so some nouveau New York actor usually moved in instead). In fact, once I took over Franny's black cocktail dress outfits and Monroe Lay starlet life, I was so busy living in Hollywood that things like garbage disposals slipped my mind.

The inside of my place was painted like a cream beach bungalow and the canvas shades were striped like beach umbrellas and all the furniture was that motel vacation furniture that made the half-a-living room next to the half-a-bedroom look like it was only someplace to change clothes before you ran back into the festivities quickly, so as not to miss a moment. (Franny's cowgirl hat was still hanging on the wall from when she lived there.)

Looking out at the green lawns of Versailles from the beachy interior of St.-Tropez made me feel so luxurious sometimes, I wanted to lie in bed propped up so I could gaze out forever, especially when it rained; when it rained in those days, Hollywood was heaven.

I had guys coming out of my ears like streetcars. Only

instead of one coming by every ten minutes, like they were supposed to, the old ones never left so my life grew dense with simultaneous romance. Lovers were like the lantana before the trellis caved in.

The first six months I went around being perfect after I started working at the Oriental, I went out to parties, gallery openings, and Barney's like there was no tomorrow and came home only to change clothes. But suddenly my desire to go out every night vanished and friends assumed love had wiped me off the scene. People were often missing who fell in love. But I was only falling into a darkroom.

Until Yorick—the Englishman who taught nuclear physics at Cal Tech at twenty-six but wanted to live in Hollywood so he could audition for cowboy parts on TV (!)—moved into the bungalow in front, cameras to me were something only a man could understand for they had too many buttons if you were only a girl.

However, Yorick took one look at some watercolors I painted and went and got his camera, insisting that understanding anything at all including mechanical buttons had nothing to do with gender.

"Let me show you a picture of my sister," he said, showing a girl in his wallet who looked like Charlotte Rampling except she wore a stethoscope. "Looking at her," he said, "you'd never think she was a surgeon."

"With a knife and everything?"

"So here's how this thing works," he began.

I mean being a surgeon made learning how to work cameras seem like child's play.

A rich child of course.

Who practiced diligently twelve hours a day.

Because it was like the piano—either you played chopsticks by only taking pictures outside at high noon, or else you could sightread something even though it had six flats and had been written in 7/16 time. And take pictures by moonlight.

And the more I knew about photographs, the better Sam's were. They practically breathed. He never indulged in being anything but right. The easier it all looked, and the more conventional the composition and subject, the less I could figure out where the light he used came from. Shadows never fell across anything, they only made lines—for definition—between fingers. My father wrote that Sam used only natural light which made me even more nonplussed, of course, until finally two or three years after I got back from Rome I called Sam's mother and drove down to her house in Boyle Heights across the street from the Evergreen Cemetery.

"Could I borrow Sam's films?" I asked.

"Who needs them," she replied. "Take them, take it all away with you—it's only using room in the garage."

His mother was four feet nine and was grating carrots for split pea soup in the kitchen when I arrived and we went out the kitchen door to the garage. All of Sam's things—shoeboxes of negatives spilling onto the greasy floor, prints curling up in crates, his reels of film I'd dragged home from Paris—were left all but forgotten against rusty rakes and hoes.

"*All* of his stuff," I asked, "you want me to take?"

"You want it?" she asked.

"Me?"

"Otherwise I'm throwing it out," she said. (She knew when threats would work.)

"When those Trotsky kids took him in," she said, "his father and I figured already he died—we were Stalinists, we'd been loyal before anyone—he knew what he was doing but all he cared was your father shouldn't laugh at him. And those other friends of his."

"Oh," I said.

Everything of Sam's was in my car. When I got back to Hollywood that evening, Yorick showed the films with Sam's synchronized 3-D movie projectors, although it made us feel ridiculous sitting there wearing those cardboard 3D glasses (which Sam had a boxful of).

But his movies were more alive than autumn leaves, objects swirled by in 3D and flew into the Dizzy Gillespie sound track like they were One.

The next day I called a friend in New York and he called a guy from the Museum of Modern Art who saw Sam's movies the next time he came to L.A. and took them back.

But of course Sam would have become a star sooner or later because anyone could have remembered how great he was—and my God, I didn't even know him before, whereas all his friends always knew he was a genius when he was alive, short or not.

Anyway, prints of Sam's picture of my father's hand eventually began costing as much as a Man Ray—that same photograph Sam took in the front yard when I watched them drape the black velvet over the chair, *that* cost three hundred dollars in this gallery in New York.

"You know," I told Ophelia when I first began taking pictures, "maybe Sam really wasn't so bad—deep down."

"Not so *bad!*" Ophelia cried. "*Ha!* Do you know that Lola and Aunt Helen once drove down to L.A. from San Francisco together after Sam went to Paris and compared notes about how mean he was to them? Aunt Helen was in love with him before she started having a nervous breakdown—*he* left *her.*"

"I know," I said, "Lola said they never laughed so hard in their lives comparing whether he made them scrub the toilet the same way."

Ophelia had married a philosopher from UCLA. His name was Jerome, he had red hair, and he was getting his Ph.D. in scientific philosophy which he tried to explain to me one time on mescaline (both of us), but although he explained it perfectly and I understood it perfectly at the time, the next morning when we were having pancakes at Ship's in Westwood, the whole thing escaped me.

In my opinion, Ophelia only married Jerome because I was in Europe and not there to throw her in the trunk of my car and drive her to Palm Springs until she saw the light. He was the epitome of white folks and everything that wasn't Watts. (Ophelia was never even able to stand rhythm and blues.) His skin was so pink his eyelashes looked like the Easter bunny. If he had even bumped into me by accident, I would have broken out in hives. He was Molly Craven's brother's son, from Harvard.

They moved to a cute little house on Fourth Street in Santa Monica with a string of red Irish setters (much darker than his hair) which kept getting run over one by one crossing Fourth Street which was no place for anything as stupid as an Irish setter to be allowed out, but Jerome always did —just like he allowed Ophelia to take photography. They lived four blocks from the house Lola and Sam lived in the first two years when Lola was still happy as a clam, not in love with Sam even then and before they got married and wrecked everything.

Whenever Ophelia and Jerome invited me over to dinner, it was always so I could wreck everything by getting married to one of their awful friends—guys from UCLA who Jerome always tried to fix me up with—but the only reason I even went was to talk Ophelia into a divorce.

"What are you doing with this person who makes you wear cameos!" I used to ask before dinner, when we went to her bedroom and smoked a joint (during the days when Jerome deplored drugs, not after he found out and changed his mind).

"He doesn't *make* me wear cameos," Ophelia exhaled,

laughing, "he gave this to me for my birthday—it was his mother's. *Jeez!*"

"Look at that dress," I cried, looking at her gray frock which buttoned up to her neck with a Peter-Pan collar underneath her Peter-Pan face, which was much too pointy and terrified and drawn in those days to go on top of a dress like that. "It makes you look like a shrunken head."

"Don't you ever want children?" Ophelia asked, looking like a shrunken head.

"*Me?*"

I got up and looked out the window at the Buicks and Oldsmobiles and Austin-Healys and MGs whip by on Fourth Street where the sun had made everything so hot that day and now was gone, leaving everything hot and barren. Part of the thing about artistic temperament in those days was women who had it didn't dare risk their lives having children around—since everybody on earth expected you to do something with them all day and not just see them around dinnertime like you would if you were most men. So rather than let them wander around Fourth Street like an Irish setter the way Jerome would, it was better to be barren and just have fun.

"But what if I get pregnant," Ophelia said.

"We can go to Tijuana," I said (planning an abortion out of motor reflex).

"But what if I want to try having a baby," Ophelia sighed, in the darkness of the room.

"Try?" I asked. "But it's so . . . terminal!"

"Oh, Sophie," she laughed, "how well put."

"Well," I said, "I'd much rather 'try' sitting. If you don't mind."

The sulphury-smelling air from the misty oil wells now cut through the past forever since if Ophelia were going to try having a baby, I'd try and lump Jerome and not think of him as her first ex-husband. Although I already knew he was.

Even though I could see how Jerome looked to Ophelia

—like *not Watts*—in her eyes for a while, one morning she was going to start drinking straight vodka, slither into a flimsy floozy dress, and follow her nose down to someplace cool.

She had a voice like a ruthless baby and I hoped one day it would escape. Or *she* would escape. (Of course after I took her backstage at the Cheetah to meet Jim and she disappeared with him for three days, she at least got away from Jerome.)

The trouble with Harry was that Jerome introduced me to him, because otherwise I'm positive I could have taken him to heart that night at once. There were all sorts of things about him that weren't too bad, like even that first night for dinner when Jerome fixed us up, Harry didn't come over empty-handed—he brought a damp bag of chocolate chip cookies (with kif in them) and about two inches of 45s, records like "Death of an Angel" and Little Julian Herrera songs. And he bought a gallon of Italian Swiss Colony Vin Rosé which he insisted we drink at room temperature— which, since it was 108 degrees that night, was only possible if you took a handful of Romilar which, it turned out, Harry supplied.

I held a handful of Romilar, but I didn't take them right away, but said, "What's this do?"

"Ooooooo," he beamed (he looked like an angelic Hell's Angel). "Nice, nice, nice. Synthetic morphine."

I took them.

"You mean they just sell these things in stores?" I asked, staring at the label (this was before they were withdrawn from the market and the synthetic morphine was eliminated about three months later; they looked like little sequin-shaped mustard pills). I took twenty or thirty.

If only a relative of Molly's hadn't been instrumental in me meeting Harry, I'm sure I would have inspired him then and there. But I had to wait three days to finally kiss him, such a taboo blocked Harry.

Anyway, how could I love at first sight anyone going to UCLA. Even if he did look like a juvenile delinquent.

The next day Ophelia called me up and said, "Well?"

"Oh, God," I said, "what time is it? My brains are falling out."

"He's the most brilliant guy in the whole school," Ophelia said, "it's all a pose, Jerome says, those chains and drugs. He's not really crazy."

"Oh," I said.

It was nearly time to get myself presentable enough to retreat to the Oriental—if I ever could remember the right change for a five-dollar bill through my hangover.

"Did you like him?" Ophelia asked.

"I don't know," I replied, "Jerome's friends, they're all so square."

The summer Harry and I met when he was an intern at UCLA, he opened four art galleries all over L.A. and changed his major to Art History, which Jerome insists was my fault.

"He could have been a brilliant surgeon!" Jerome said.

"Well," I explained, "I mean, I thought he really knew what he was doing to have been able to look like that."

"So for that he wrecks his whole future?" Jerome cried. "What did you say to him anyway?"

"I wanted him to open a restaurant," I explained, "but he took it the wrong way. He must have had this art stuff in the back of his mind all along."

Six months later, Harry dropped out of UCLA entirely and got a job as an assistant museum curator and started wearing *suits!*

"But Harry, we can't go see The Byrds at the Trip on their first night back in L.A. with you in a fucking suit!!!" I said, when he came to pick me up. "Everybody'll think you're my father!! Look how short my skirt is, I'm not going out in this mini with you like that!!!"

(But of course I had to, I mean it was too late to make his hair any longer if we were going to get there to see Paul Butterfield, the opening act.)

Harry was consistent about one thing from the very beginning and that was art—for not only did he know about it, he knew what he liked. (He'd been ravaged by seeing some kind of Marcel Duchamp collection in Pasadena when he was little and unbeknownst to anyone had been a prisoner ever since.) And he never referred to my photographs as "nice little snaps."

"No wonder I didn't think I could ever fuck you," I said to him. "You take everything so *seriously!!!* You act like I need a bedside manner—you act like everybody does!"

"This is my favorite," Harry said, regarding my favorite too—a photograph I took of all these criss-crossed palm trees growing in different directions on Foothill (right near where Lola wore her blue taffeta dress).

"It's only for sentimental value," I said, blushing, his eyes were such radar, I was afraid he'd pick up the scent practically.

Embracing Harry for dear life on the back of his motorcycle the night he drove me home from Jerome and Ophelia's was as close as I ever came to a genuine Jewish doctor like my grandmother from Kiev hoped I'd marry.

March 3, 1962

Dear Momser and Pomser,

Why are you staying in Heidelberg so long? When are you coming home? You can live in the Pagoda Chateau— really, Heidelberg's so full of chilblains.

Love,
Sophie-Pophie

March 15, 1962

Darling dear:

Your father and I have just come back from Spain where
we visited some very nice friends of the Jameses' who
own a lovely castle on the Côte d'Azur and we ate, and ate
and ate. Your father will stay here for another year gathering material for his magnum opus. This summer will
find us in Fiesole—your sister will be with us, you can
drop by too if it's not out of your way. Bonnie seems to be
learning French and Frenchmen.

> Your
> Ma

Letters like the two above started in 1962 when I came
back from Rome and went on for about ten years. My parents
seemed satisfied just to stay in castles and eat, plus go to
Venice for little potatoes which my mother was crazy about
and white truffles from Milan in December, which kept her
stuck there like glue. My father kept getting extensions on
his Ford Foundation grant and since there seemed to be an
unending source of Bachiana in Marburg (twelve k's from
Heidelberg), he didn't care if it was snowing or raining or
whether he got taquitos or anything.

They did come back once—just once—in 1966 when my
father was invited to direct a seminar at Cal Tech one summer on Early Music—and he had these little concerts every
fortnight where all the people who'd drive to Pasadena for a
concert of Palestrina would go, mostly the little old ladies
who still lived there (the kind who used to frown on the
movie colony and thought Hollywood was just a bunch of
gypsies in tents).

(Maybe we were, but my parents were gypsies at least in
castles.)

As I look back on myself (now that I'm older and dimmer), I must have been nuts because Harry was the most stable force in my life—and Harry wasn't any too stable a force even when they imported him to New York and made him a museum director (where everyone working with him wore buttons saying "Harry Will Be Back in 20 Minutes" since nobody ever knew where he was).

But the other guys, like Maurice, who got busted for kilos of grass in a bass fiddle case, or Douglas, the actor from London who looked like a lad of seventeen until his wife and five children appeared, or Ron, the TV cowboy star who was six feet five inches and rode around in a metallic Kelly-green Cadillac convertible to match his eyes until he decided to go to Ireland where he heard the whole place was Kelly green (returning a shell of his former self from the rain), or Grant, who taught acting only I couldn't act so when we fell in love doom was in the air: compared to guys like that, Harry was a pillar of the community.

And I was an L.A. woman. In fact, looking back on those one-night stands, I must have been crazy. Yet there were thousands of girls living between Sunset and Santa Monica in between La Brea and La Cienega who painted the town red like me—and who got away with it too.

It wasn't as though I were alone.

But then there were girls of course who painted the town red and didn't get away with it. I mean, there was a darker side to life, for some girls, no matter how hard they tried, were always going to be ladies (my idea of the darker side).

And the next thing after that was victims. I mean, if you were a lady, you were a sitting duck from then on.

Being a lady did fascinate me. It happened, sometimes, to the best people—like maybe when Lola had collapsed into propriety and married Sam. Somehow, for me, myself, it never occurred to me even out of the clear blue sky. Like once when I went to New York to see Harry, I was standing in front of the gallery, when two rotten little six-foot-two teenagers flew by and grabbed my purse when nothing but my driver's license—not money—was in it. Before they'd gotten fifteen feet away, I said, "There's no money, really, look."

(They stopped and looked, they were so surprised.)

"Leave it," I said, "I need my driver's license."

So they did. (But then, teenagers I understand, especially rotten ones.)

Or another morning when I woke up in bed with this man sitting on top of me holding his hand over my mouth saying, "Don't scream." Naturally I screamed, although I really wanted to make him stay and explain how he had become a rapist in this day and age—only by then he had climbed out the window saying "Oh, shit." (As though I were the wet blanket.)

Ladies and victims never reason with teenaged purse-snatchers or rapists and that's why I knew I wasn't one.

Sheila, a girl my age who went to L.A. High and lived next to me in the court, worked part time in a travel agency and looked like a Botticelli—and she was worse than me. I mean, when I moved into that court and had tea with Sheila the first day, we decided to list all the men we had slept with—we were both not twenty-one yet—only I forgot their names after counting 50 I remembered, and Sheila got to 150 (she could even remember last names) before she got confused.

Stuff like jealousy and outrage and sexual horror tactics like that, which had been used to squash girls like us and keep us from having fun for thousands of years, now suddenly didn't stand a chance because Sheila and the rest of us weren't going to get pregnant, die of syphilis, or get horrible reputations around L.A.—where an L.A. woman had always pretty much painted the town anything she wanted.

And anyway stuff like jealousy was too late if you were going to be in love with Jim.

And if you were me, you would.

There he was in a dark nightclub I'd gone one night when I was twenty-three and he was twenty-two and poetry was curling around him like smoke. He smelled like leather and alcohol and nightclubs but he looked blind like a marble statue. Outside was the Sunset Strip but inside he was living on borrowed time. And I was wearing gardenias.

It was 1966 and I wanted the whole thing. Fast.

We were being introduced by someone normal, the only thing normal about us.

"Let's go," I said.

His voice broke the silence like putting a card on a house of cards, and he said, "Go?"

"Yeah," I said, "to my house."

"I'm with the band," he said.

"Oh, don't tell me we have to wait till after you play!"

"I don't play," he said, "I work."

In those days I used to think that love at first sight and happiness were the same thing.

But after love at first sight with Jim I noticed that although he was much taller than Sam and in fact even though I was now taller than Sam, I felt the same way about Jim as I once had with Sam which was—Not Woman Enough.

No matter how high my heels were, I could very easily have been with Sam if I shut my eyes.

Of course, trying to be woman enough for someone who couldn't even get enough woman if he lived to be a hundred and *six* was impossible—it was like volunteering for astronaut school—I mean, you knew there were thousands of other just-as-qualified volunteers ready to follow him anywhere, only as the groupie pool deepened, there were always ones who'd follow him anywhere, only naked, or in a mink coat, or with hair like fire.

But then, once I realized he liked hair like fire, I did mine red too. In fact, I looked untamed and restless enough in the clothes I went out in for Genghis Khan and Ivan the Terrible put together. But looking woman enough was so hard—having to pincurl my hair so it would look art nouveau-y (which you *had* to look—in a brutal sort of way, of course) and *being* woman enough when you're on acid was just . . . I mean, walking out on the balcony of the Tropicana at 4:00 A.M. Sunday morning with Jim—naked—was just . . . I mean, I could see his point, it *was* cool—but I was chicken. That was the long and the short of it. Just not woman enough.

And even if I *won*, like Lola, and actually did get to make breakfast for him forever—all I kept remembering was my mother the time she watched Lola making Sam breakfast in San Francisco when he dumped his eggs in the garbage and said, "I can't eat this—you can't even scramble eggs!"

At which point my mother told Lola to sit down and proceeded to make breakfast herself, ". . . and he didn't dare talk that way to *me*," she said, "I mean, hell, in Texas men knew how to be a devil, they didn't sit around complaining about scrambled eggs. Now my uncle, he was a high fuck—"

"A what?" I asked.

"And listen," she ended, "my mother married guys like Sam, but they were *real!*"

Until I met Jim the pictures I took were so artsy they weren't art but I was so mad at *his* L.A., his Symptom of the Apocalypse attitude, that every picture I began to take was proof he was wrong—and they really *worked*. They were casual, but in an obsessed kind of way since I wanted to make L.A. look as though even a child could see that the bungalows and palm trees were only bungalows and palm trees and not out to kill the rest of the world. And that the papier-mâché shacks built forty years earlier by a swindler weren't a swindle, because people were still merrily living in them and waiting for something to knock them over with a feather—snow, never mind an apocalypse.

And I got so casual that I became a professional and quit the Oriental the day I got my first check for three hundred dollars for an album cover, which I thought was a fortune.

By the time I quit the Oriental Jim was a star and I was a free-lance photographer actually getting checks for pictures because I got so casual I could even pass for professional. But I was much too scared of Jim to ever take his picture.

The trouble with Jim was that he was so much worse in person that I stayed in shock until he left. His silences were so much more deadly, the elliptical remarks so much emptier, and the nonstop fury within him to capture the world's imagination was so religious and dignified and ironical that, like pain, you only remembered what it was like when it was too late.

In retrospect of course he seemed worth it.

In fact, from afar he was gorgeous. But he was too gorgeous in bed to be true, except if you wanted to borrow some of his borrowed time, which you might never get out of. (With Jim the end was at hand every night, and dawn was never a given.)

Someone once told me that greatness was a disease. And that must have been what was wrong with Jim. (Among other things.)

It was strange because in the middle of all that intensity when Jim was actually there in person, Ed Lakey was all I could think about. Ed Lakey kissing me in La Coupole and promising to make me a star—I mean, at least Ed let someone else be a star now and then. With Jim no one else was allowed to capture imaginations but him. He got so pissed off when someone else was a star that once when he was standing next to Janis Joplin at a party he yanked her hair so hard, she broke a bottle of Southern Comfort over his head and he had to go to the emergency hospital. The next night I sat across from her in Barney's when Jim came in and I heard her say, "Do you think he's still mad at me?"

She almost sounded like she hoped he was.

But he wasn't still mad except at his head being bandaged. So if she thought he'd be perfect for the guy in the Billie Holiday song who kicked girls down the stairs, she was sadly mistaken.

Maybe some people come into the world thinking things are too small and they can't do anything unless it's enormous, and like Jim the trouble was trying to find something enormous enough to leave a mark *with*—perhaps an eight-foot-high pencil—but that still didn't make the person pushing the pencil the right size.

Before I figured all this out, no matter when he called me I always knew those silences even before he said hello and had my shoes on and my car keys and was ready to go pick him up from the Troubador and lie there next to him all night still in all my clothes, just to make sure nobody took too many reds. And that there was a next day.

But then L.A. was filled with women keeping him alive— West Hollywood was a net to break his fall. He was passed from hand to hand like a trophy. And since he at least knew enough not to drive a car, he was always out there in the noonday smog on foot waiting for girls to seduce him.

Jim wasn't real like guys from Texas. All he was was real for L.A.

For L.A., in fact, he was too real.

My friend Suzannah, who lived down the street in an overgrown Eden court with stained glass windows and a lily pond down the middle, came from Laguna Beach where she was so adorable that nobody knew she was pregnant when she graduated from Laguna Beach High and nobody knew she had run down to Tijuana to one of the clinics with her sister afterwards, when they wondered where she was at the graduation party. She began going to UCLA the next semester, where she was so wholesome and enthusiastic and sweet

that she was captured by a spy from Rogers and Cowan, the
P.R. firm in Beverly Hills that handled movie stars mostly,
and given a job making three hundred dollars a week taking
the Rolling Stones on tour throughout America all by herself
—when she was nineteen.

("Thrown to the wolves," she called it.)

Suzannah tried to make herself look older by dressing in
beige and having her hair streaked silver and gold, but with
her platinum pink toenails, she always reminded me more of
the girl friend of a retired gangster. And with me in my blue
and black chintz embroidered twenties pajamas and my
blond hair rinsed orange by henna, the two of us together
struck most people as a coincidence, when in truth we were
almost inseparable, at least when we went off to the Sunset
Strip at night.

During the daytime, Suzannah was at work and I too
would wake up and do things all day, like work too. In between running around with stranded friends, all I did all day
was develop pictures, print prints, run back and forth to art
directors, drag every single person I ever met around L.A.
with me so they wouldn't feel bereft—especially strangers
from Texas and New York (since people from London,
France, and Italy seemed to expect L.A. to be exactly like it
was), taking them downtown and to Pasadena and to the
beach and to all my favorite friends' houses and introducing
everybody I knew to everybody else so they wouldn't feel
catatonic—and so my older L.A. friends wouldn't stagnate
up in their Laurel Canyon peace and quiet (none of *my*
friends *ever* had much peace and quiet). I would throw parties at the drop of a hat when I made enough money to move
to the Spanish duplex down the street (which when the people who rented it to me wanted to know how come a single
girl would want it, since it was a two-bedroom, I had to
explain it was because I needed the space for "my work"—
although the next thing they knew, I had a party for sixty

people in jeans, and limos and falling-apart hearses were parked and double-parked up and down the whole street). I refused to have parties I didn't cook for since from my own experience I'd found that no matter how wonderful a party was, if the food seemed rented—catered chili or lasagna— the party made a hollow impression; whereas if the food was totally unexpected and *great* (like I cooked, but then, I did inherit *some*thing from my mother besides her voice—although everybody who got us mixed up on the phone never would have mistaken my parties for hers because my friends had much longer hair), then no matter how awful everything else was, people still left feeling like they'd gotten away with murder.

Of course people at my parties were often convinced landing-in-paradise was for hippies or "peace and love" victims so whatever I did to the food, it had to be all over with after one little taste. I roasted two entire turkeys and made cornbread stuffing drenched in Grand Marnier with sausages, oysters, chestnuts, and apricots. After they "just tasted" one bite of my stuffing, it was too late of course and if they wanted to feel hollow after that, they'd obviously have to wait a few days. Fortunately food I had anything to do with was always like knockout drops—only instead of you passing out, all anybody did was pass *up* into divine gluttony.

Divine gluttony of course was out of fashion. In fact, by the time my two turkeys made their mark it was 1968 and gluttony had become extinct everywhere in the known world where trying to be skinny like the Beatles, or really skinny like George Harrison, had left the civilized world between thirteen and thirty on a food-free vacation. Some friends preferred to think my ulterior motive behind making dolmas for two days was a trick to make them feel good.

"You're always trying to make people feel at ease!" one of my uncomplicated men friends argued—but men were always accusing me of having fun.

But most people if you asked me always were warning me not to have fun for my own good and were curious to see what became of me if I refused to stop believing some of my friends would turn out to be quite so wonderful once I was in the gutter with a crust of bread.

"My friends will always be utterly fabulous," I'd say, totally convinced that except for this one problem my friends had about how rotten they were going to be—or at least how rotten everybody else I raved about (like I raved about them of course to everyone else) was just one more person I befriended for all the wrong reasons and not really like them at all.

"Is that Suzannah a friend of yours," a man wanted to know, "or what?"

The minute a check arrived from the record companies I'd leave enough for my rent and spend the rest instantly having a party. Of course I was always broke. And I got broker. And broker.

"What you need is some man—" women explained.

"Some *man!*" I cried. "What for?"

"To pay for everything," one older woman explained.

"But I'd be too depressed to *buy* anything," I said.

"Some older man," she went on, ignoring my seeming disinterest, ". . . with money, who thinks everything you do is okay. And doesn't mind you."

"But all men mind me!" I tried to explain, since they all did. "No guy's going to just sit there reading a book while I'm off someplace far enough to spend his money in peace. I'm too easily led astray. This guy would have to not mind philandering if he was just so great—and I know this guy isn't that great."

"Well," she said, "what are you going to do?"

"Do?"

It still confused people that I was practically twenty-six years old and they had no firm picture of my life, which I didn't either except that lately I knew enough to wake up and take as many pictures everyday as I could before Suzannah and I went out looking for trouble (which by then we'd practiced looking for too long not to find every last drop). During the day, though, my photographs were all I believed I was doing, so I did have some firm picture of what I did and just so long as I took firm pictures myself, I was being an artist—and I didn't need to know anything more about my life—and even if it was a horrible way to make money, starving was what artists did.

I wasn't starving, because practically everybody I knew had an expense account, and the only thing I spent money on besides parties and rent and the phone was film which wasn't cheap and printing film which wasn't even cheaper. Of course, if worse came to worse, there were always men; men always seemed made out of money to me. I looked upon men, in those days, as people who'd never miss my incredibly reasonable fifty dollars for cabfare which was much too cheap to make me feel like a hooker. (But then being a hooker seemed more like a good idea every day. Especially at the Beverly Hills Hotel. In fact, being a hooker seemed a far more brilliant idea than having to really get married and breaking my spirit completely. Even when I was ten years old before I even heard of Sam, it seemed obvious to me that getting all dressed up in slinky clothes and being out every night and having men pay you was much more brilliant than getting stuck doing dishes at home every night with nobody to talk to except *him*—and since I already seemed to be wearing slinky clothes and going out every night anyway, it sometimes seemed such a shame to call myself a photographer.)

In fact, by then I knew I was getting too old to be a record album photographer. I was losing my groupie touch and had begun telling rock'n'roll stars I hated rock'n'roll and nobody is that cute. "I wonder what happens to grown men when they get to be thirty and all they know how to do is rock'n'roll," I started to wonder out loud.

"Great," Sheila the Botticelli sighed, "here's a knife, if you want to slit your throat just go ahead. But *do* it! Just get the good part over with where I can watch. There's Jim, why don't you ask him what he's going to do when he's thirty. But then he's not going to live that long. . . ."

We were sitting against the wall in the Troubador Bar and Sheila and I were having double margaritas on the rocks and I was already on my fourth so the room had blended into everybody there and we were all one except Jim who saw me and the one-arm bandit in his head was pulled into compute and he opened both eyes which were the same color and leveled out into equal hopelessness which seemed as close to the jackpot as his eyes ever came and suddenly the rest of his face was alive.

And he smiled.

In fact, he smiled and made his way toward me through the bar even though he was torn from groupies the whole fifteen feet by the time he got to us, and he politely mumbled if he could sit down and I had the chair under him in time to break his fall.

"My God, Jim, *what* are you drinking?" I asked.

"Uh hi," he said, blending into the bar for a moment before fading away again.

"Jim, go *home!*" I suggested. "You're just making yourself look like a ridiculous rock star to get publicity. And you're *too old* for this!"

But suddenly I realized that I was a year older and suddenly I realized that I couldn't love Jim like this—it was too expensive.

Suddenly I realized everyone *was* too old for the way we were behaving. And for a moment it was like a nasty shock that you couldn't get over because it was true—everybody at our corner was at least twenty-five and they all knew it was too old. But across the room I saw two boys who didn't look too old to me after all because they looked too young and callow but anything was better I thought than my table and as I lurched to my feet I said, "Anything's better than you guys."

"Take your knife," Sheila suggested, but I was really beginning to think Sheila had lost her sense of humor, the things she was always talking about: knives—my wrecked career—killing myself every time I opened my mouth—it was so boring trying to have a rational conversation anymore, my God.

"Hi," I slyly floated into new blood.

"*Well* hel*lo!*" one said, making it sound as though *he* was trying to pick *me* up instead of the other way around—out of politeness.

"Hi," the second innocent young man also said, "you want to sit down?"

"Let's," I decided, wedging in between them at the bar and being offered the one barstool left at the too-crowded bar.

Their names were Glen and J.D. they said, and I said, "Mine's Sophie Lubin."

"*The* Sophie Lubin." Glen's eyes suddenly widened in awe.

"*The* Sophie Lubin?" I asked. "Who's that?"

"Oh," J.D. said, "we thought you were the Sophie Lubin who designs album covers—you know, the one who takes pictures, who's famous—but you have almost exactly the same-sounding name, so we thought you were *the* Sophie Lubin!"

"And when we make our first album, she's who we're gonna get," Glen proudly added. "She's the *best*."

In my opinion, the only way my album covers ever worked was by my being a groupie and blazing with tenderness over what idols my idols were and for me to regard Glen and J.D. as anything but sensible young men with taste enough to idolize *me* was too much to ask.

In fact, at twenty-seven everything I did was rejected and I lived on kill fees—one third of their usual three hundred or five hundred dollars, when they shouldn't pay you anything. Kill fees seem almost too kind.

I decided to put off being a hooker just until it turned out I couldn't write either even though everybody always said my letters showed how talented I could be if I tried—art directors rejecting my work *especially* advised me to be a writer. Since I was eight I always knew I'd be a writer if all else failed.

(And once *that* failed, I'd always wanted to be a hooker too. There were plenty of things I could do.)

EVERYTHING I'VE ALWAYS HEARD about Geminis reminds me of me—mercurial, dualistic, schizy. But I'm actually a Taurus and they're supposed to be bovine, stubborn, and single-minded. So you can see what a strain it always was for me since I was all these things: dualistic and single-minded. But as Gandhi once said, "I'd rather be right than consistent."

I sent Franny a screenplay in Rome (which took me a year to write but it was something to do while I was waiting for checks from record companies), it seemed like *fun*. So when Ed sent me a check for five thousand dollars which he said was an "option," you could have knocked me over with a feather. But I was always lucky.

"Don't show this to anyone else," Ed explained in person, when he and Franny flew in from Colorado looking like Ivory Soap commercials, in spite of all their suede and ermine-lined gloves.

"Ed's so paranoid," Franny said, "he's afraid somebody's going to steal your idea."

"Idea? It's just the cheapest thing to shoot, that's all, a love story—except instead of boy meets girl, loses girl, gets girl —it's boy gets girl, loses girl. Girl gets better boy. And original boy dies."

(It was a sort of rough artistic license version of Lola and Sam and Luther.)

"I know, but it's a comedy," Franny said, "it's never been done before, a bedroom farce where the hero blows it so badly no one will miss him."

"What do you *mean*, comedy!" I cried. "Not *miss* him? *That's* not how to make a martini!"

"What?"

"You know, that joke about martinis," I said, "how this guy tries to make a martini only there's always somebody looking over his shoulder telling him more vermouth or less lemon peel, so finally he flies to Arabia and rents a camel and rides out into the desert for a day and a half till finally there's no one as far as the eye can see—and he gets down off the camel, takes out the gin, the vermouth, the ice cubes, the shaker, the glass, and just as he's measuring the vermouth, this voice from God booms out: 'That's not how to make a martini.' "

"So?" Franny wondered. "What's that got to do with anything?"

"Oh nothing," I said, not wanting to sound like a writer saying, "That's not what my screenplay's about!" just because I'd accidentally been mistaken for one after all I'd done was write something—I mean any minute it seemed I might be blurting something like "Producers are all assholes" if I didn't look out and turn into one of those ridiculous people for good, which scared me so much I almost forgot it was July and the five thousand dollars had doubled my income for the whole year—at least so far. I calmed down. I mean, I realized that I didn't have to be consistent and behave like a writer just because they were right. In fact, nobody could tell me I was bovine and stubborn when I was obviously split like the schiziest Gemini all over the place, because now not only did I have to seem so accidentally spontaneous nobody would suspect I was trying to be good, I also had to trick myself into writing without being a writer. On the other hand, I got an agent.

A friend of Ed's named Nan Kamp.

Even though whenever my latest car, a '57 Plymouth station wagon, stopped it had a death rattle, I picked up Franny in front of the sweeping grandeur of the Beverly Hills Hotel because I figured I was rich enough not to have to *look* rich once Ed made a deal with Paramount so we could all go to the seashore.

"You wanna go to Kelbo's?" Franny asked. "It's dark."

Before, we used to have to go dark places when we didn't want anyone to notice we were fifteen. Now we were old enough, only Franny was a star and you couldn't take her anywhere people didn't notice except if it was pitch black.

"Why don't you fucking go incognito?" I complained. "No wonder everyone notices when you have that mouth with you. Couldn't you eat popsicles in public?"

"They melt," she explained, "and turn my tongue raspberry."

Inside Kelbo's we got our usual table and were lost in gloom like we were when we were vicious virgins—only we ordered champagne since Uncle George no longer made Vicious Virgins anymore after he got busted.

"Before the champagne arrives," Franny said, "let's get the house out of the way."

"House?"

"You know, my old house—the one I owe you for making me a star."

"The one with the wisteria and the fourteen rooms and the fountains that even worked and the cracked tennis court?" I asked.

"Yes, here are the keys," she said, "and this envelope, be careful with because it's got all the deed stuff from the real estate lady in it."

She handed me keys and a large brown envelope.

"But Franny," I said, "I didn't make you a star, you already *were* a star only nobody knew."

"Ahhh, champagne," she sighed, as our waiter poured us two glasses. She lifted hers in a toast and I was dumbfounded but lifted mine anyway.

"But what about your parents?" I asked.

"I got our old house back in Bel Air and they're home," she said. "Now let's toast . . . to—"

"But I didn't make you a star, *Ed* made you a star," I said.

"He had no choice," she said. "When you stood him up in Rome, the wardrobe was already finished and he *had* to find someone the same size right away—I had the only tits big enough."

"Oh," I said, "in that case, we earned it."

"Let's toast something deserving," Franny said, "to . . ."

". . . tits," I suggested, since she seemed stumped.

"To tits," she agreed, clinking her glass to mine. We sipped.

"Can I have your autograph?" someone lost in the gloom wondered.

We never even got to finish one glass.

"On the other hand," I said, "we could drink to all the tits we want at my parents' house—let's get some champagne To Go."

When we got there, we paused for a moment on the balcony overlooking the living room (which still had beebee holes in it from Franny's father shooting the brass Liberty Bell), and Franny said, "God, this place is so big, everybody in L.A. could sit down."

"Yeah," I said, "once we get chairs."

We turned on the fountains, which still worked, and toasted each room, eating pineapple guavas from a tree I hadn't seen there before, until we ended up at twilight in the dining room.

"Maybe I can find that rose wallpaper and make this place look more like home for their homecoming present," I said.

"Oh look," Franny said. "She's still there."

From where we stood, we could see all the way to the top of the Taft Building at Hollywood and Vine where the Millers Beer sign had just gone on—with the lady swinging from the moon to and fro, to and fro, while neon stars twinkled on and off, on and off. Of course most nights you can't see real stars over L.A. because it's too misty, but I had seen those from my bedroom window when I was little so I knew what authentic stars were like—and even then I always liked ours better.

Epilogue

Lola and Luther had come down for my parents' homecoming party and the house was filled with requited sweetpeas even though it was the hottest day of the year in the wrong month—June. Everything trembled like babies' fingernails before the guests came and my mother looked like being back in Hollywood at last filled her with the pink light she liked to breathe in.

My father now looked like Einstein played by Leslie Howard and he was playing the violin in the middle of the living room while my grandmother (who stopped minding my mother soon after the scissors incident) and Goldie kept avoiding him to put more glasses on the coffee table.

Bonnie had veered into L.A. from New York where being

the white sheep of the family was no longer an embarrassment since she was a union organizer like my grandfather and had found a station in life which fit in with something we understood.

Ophelia was married to a jazz musician named Art with black wavy hair and that slightly blast-off look in his eyes.

Even my Japanese girl friend from junior high, Ollie, was there.

And I was wearing my Miss Niagara Falls sequined thing that the lady in the antique store said belonged to Marlene Dietrich and was seven hundred dollars in the Depression because each and every sequin was sewn on by hand and the thing shot light out like one of those mirrored chandeliers. Of course you couldn't sit down in it or the sequins all went at right angles to your ass but until I sat down I didn't know that.

Here I was just two years beyond twenty-six when no one knew why I wasn't married, and now Harry and Ed were coming, so in case anybody like my Aunt Lily wanted to persuade me to become a physical therapist again or my friend Frank got frantic trying to talk me into becoming a computer programmer or Francie, who kept on about the older man who wouldn't mind me, came by, I could always find at least one person to vouch for my obsessions paying off.

But then even if they hadn't, I realized, I wouldn't love my obsessions any less.

And Lola and I went for a walk up Canyon Drive to stand in front of her old house hanging on a hill almost invisible from evergreen branches and I didn't love *her* obsessions any less either.

"But why did you marry him?" I began.

"Because really I had nothing else to do," she said.

"I left New York, my boyfriend there was very cute, but not smart enough," she said—we both looked up to the top of this ancient tree which her mother must have planted—

"and when I came back to L.A. he was waiting for me. He wouldn't get off my front porch. He was crazy about me and he wouldn't leave me alone. And I had nothing else to do."

"You didn't?" I asked.

"I didn't know what to do with myself if I wasn't a dancer," she said, "and there I was getting older. There wasn't anything else I could do."

"But God, Lola, those *guys*. . . ."

"I *know*, those guys!" she said. "But you should have seen the *others!*"

"My father at least let my mother have fun," I said, "all the others picked them off like candles with a snuffer."

"Your father only plays Bach!"

"You know I have brains enough for two, if a guy lets you have fun why should he play anything or have any brains anyway—and all they do when they're smart is *suffer*."

"But not as much as you suffer," she said, "but I suppose that's why they're smart."

"You know my father used to listen to those guys like Sam and he'd go around for a month saying how remarkable it was that there were no great women artists."

"*Oi gevalt*," Lola said.

"Only then, we were on our way to Sante Fe and he takes us sixty miles out of our way and takes us to go see Georgia O'Keeffe in the middle of nowhere because she's so great."

"You don't say."

"I was twelve, my God, was that like a bolt of something that worked."

"Her work is beautiful."

"But you know I used to wander down Hollywood Boulevard hoping that Georgia O'Keeffe wasn't really just a man by accident because she was the only woman artist, period, but then, you know, I told my mother, and she told me Marilyn Monroe was an artist and not to worry. And so I realized she was right and didn't."

"My favorite was Marlene, oooooo, what a face," Lola said (she looked like Marlene more every day).

"But *why* did you marry Sam?" I wondered.

"Because I had nothing else to do."

My grandmother from Kiev had a genius for changing her mind.

One minute Goldie was a child prodigy too talented to do anything but dance, the next Goldie was like a knife in her mother's heart still not married and twenty already.

Or one minute all my father's high school friends were angels and "smart too," and the next they were "peasants."

Of course she was so engaging during Part I that she had to be right during Part II as well and it was through rude awakenings that you were putty in her hands.

"She must have hated Sam," I said to my father, that day at the party after my walk with Lola.

"Oh, no," he quickly replied, "Sam she couldn't hate because he was too beautiful."

"Too beautiful!" I exclaimed. "Nobody told me he was *that* beautiful. If Grandma couldn't hate him, he really did something to people, didn't he?"

(I mean, beauty was the only thing my grandmother couldn't see through. But then I had the same blind spot myself.)

"Oh yes," my father said, "he was quite an attractive person."

"All I thought was that people were so stupid they let Sam be mean to them for no reason. I had no idea he was quite *that* attractive a person."

"Yeah," my father signed, "but it must have been his eyes."

Of course it wasn't his eyes, it was *him*. Now that I knew he was beautiful his eyes fell into place, for it all made sense to have people relishing lavender eyes if they were trying to explain the mystery of what he did and turn him into words like a story. But details like eyes and how mean he was to Lola were only the subplot—the main thing was that he was too beautiful for Grandma to change her mind. And *that* was beautiful.

People who saw Franny's old house after my parents moved back to L.A. thought it was our original old house sometimes and I myself sort of melded them together in time too.

I still lived in the apartment on Martel because I lived exactly where it was perfect and money had nothing to do with it; in fact writing screenplays was okay but there was something to be said for developing pictures all day long too. Plus people knew where to come if I had parties.

I think the thing everybody decided was wrong about Hollywood—the trance people seemed to live in—was really the most necessary ingredient running everything. That Neptunian blur was what made L.A. great and that Aimee Semple McPherson suspension of disbelief along with the ether mystics was really what brought movie stars to life. There is a sort of cocoon around L.A. that compelled compassion out of skeptics, but of course movies were so gigantic that everyone knew how great they were trying to be and felt sorry for them when they weren't. At least in the beginning, until the fifties, but how can you be great in color? It took Fellini to be great in color. Of course the city of Los Angeles itself scattered into the one-story horizon somehow made people wonder how seamless stories of splendid aristocracy in palaces could come from the trackless waste—but everybody who really lived in L.A. was linked into the trance. Everybody knew certain boulders were fake and they knew why.

The fake boulders and the compassion and women dancing in Grecian togas came out of the same trance too—the trance of irrevocable loss—because whatever it was, it was only a movie.

But at least movies were work.

The sky over L.A. is as flat horizontally as Africa, an Italian once told me, and he felt nervous in L.A. thinking the whole place might crack on his head. But the feeling in L.A. that the place was not safe—that hovering earthquake in the air —was why anyone in the trance even came down long enough to learn to thread a camera at all. They had to take their eye off what was probably the apocalypse and invent Theda Bara out of a girl from Cincinnati to make sense out of the light.

The world was wide open from 1916 on when too many girls were already in Hollywood, and although virgins were warned not to come to L.A., anything was better than Sour Lake. No matter what they say about the bluebird of happiness, it was not in anyone's backyard in 1933 in Texas.

Somehow the trance escaped men of vision when they wrote about L.A., because nothing struck them as wonderful about a whole town where all the girls were too beautiful and too preoccupied to do anything but work. These girls struck men as victims of Hollywood since marriage slipped their minds completely as an idea of something to do.

But even the girls who failed abysmally weren't sorry since they were part of the Big Trance of what was wrong in L.A. with the women.

I myself have never been one of those people who are so great that Hollywood destroys them. I knew we were all in the same boat the whole time rewriting that damn script, and since it was probably the *Titanic* it was just as well to be polite. Anyway, when I began with Ed and Franny at Paramount every day like they must have done before I was born when my mother said "Hollywood was Hollywood," being there was awe-inspiring enough to keep me sedated. We were inside the empire and everybody knew it.

It was what we have to remind us of Hollywood when it was wide open.

When I left Rome, of course, the inside of studios slipped from my grasp but Franny became so adept at dubbing seven or eight voices and her own, and Mitchell Craven was himself so much better than anyone else in Italy, that Ed was back in L.A. trying to talk me back into acting like love was blind or something. They all three became hot and never stopped working for one minute—always freezing or frying on some location being great during the day.

But then movies are the holy commitment people making them jump into although nobody working on a movie ever left for work before 3:00 A.M. so far as Franny ever heard. But usually 5:00 A.M. is when they start their cars in the darkness and smooth their way down Melrose in the silence. They stay there all day, waiting endlessly in the trance suspended in time, and they slip back out at twilight for a straightforward dinner and 10:00 is as late as anyone can stay awake. It's a huge tradition as devious as the Vatican and as clear as light, but they aren't going anywhere without a script so I was glad I had one.

Suddenly our particular trance turned into a monarch butterfly and everybody knew just how to make it look real. Though irrevocable loss did cling since it was only a movie.

By that time I figured maybe twenty-eight was not too old. But then there's no place like the studios to make you feel innocent by comparison.

And in the meantime Harry came out of *his* trance on the East Coast and flew into L.A. about this show he suddenly dragged me out of the studio all day and all night to do.

I couldn't believe it sitting there in my apartment when Sheila called about how Jim died in Paris. It took me two years not to see him coming around corners the way he always did, and in Barney's there was so much of him in the air.

But gradually the line he drew became too perfect not to have ended in Paris and I saw that his life could be over since it was, after all, his life and not mine. I had never liked being the subject of my art in person since actors must act, even if it kills them.

Of course normal people will think that art can be taken too far, but the trouble with being normal is it stops you from being great. And Jim knew exactly what great was.

But you know, if he'd seen Paramount, he might have been great another fifty years and never come down once.

And I wanted to take him to meet my parents, their house was right up from the Vedanta Temple north of Vine. And we could have gone into the Hollywood Cemetery in back of Paramount where my Great Aunt Golda from Kiev in her urn can look out at the painted sky overhanging the back lot. We could go look at Rudolph Valentino's crypt and think about how long it's been since the words "Must I be valet as well as lover" made Lola come for the first time.

If only the next people who decided to have a war would stay home and make a movie instead, it would be just as expensive and beyond human control, but by the time you got sick of it, you could go home.

Anyway, if you can't be Marilyn Monroe there might be something else you can do. And if a girl in blue could leave Sour Lake, Texas, simply to be around movies when Hollywood was Hollywood, then just being an L.A. woman, if you ask me, was always what Hollywood did best.